MURDER BY THE BOOK

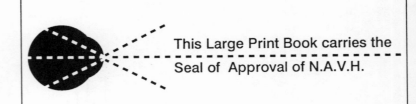

Murder by the Book

A Mr. and Mrs. North Mystery

BY
FRANCES AND RICHARD
LOCKRIDGE

Thorndike Press • Thorndike, Maine

Library of Congress Cataloging in Publication Data:

Lockridge, Frances Louise Davis.
  Murder by the book : a Mr. and Mrs. North
mystery / by Frances and Richard Lockridge.
    p.   cm.
  ISBN 1-56054-222-5 (alk. paper : lg. print)
  1. Large type books. I. Lockridge, Richard, 1898-
II. Title.
[PS3523.O243M73   1991]   91-22667
813'.54—dc20   CIP

Thorndike Press Large Print edition published in 1991 by
arrangement with HarperCollins Publishers, Inc.

Large Print edition available in the British Commonwealth
by arrangement with Curtis Brown Ltd.

Cover design by Tammy Giardello.

The tree indicium is a trademark of Thorndike Press.

This book is printed on acid-free, high opacity paper.

MURDER BY THE BOOK

I

Gerald North woke up and said, "But pelicans are birds." He said this firmly, as one might who planned to have no argument about it. He heard each word, and each word distinct, even emphatic. He had announced, to an unfamiliar ceiling, that pelicans were birds. There could be no doubt of this. He rather wished there might be.

He turned on his side and looked at the next bed, in which Pamela North should be lying. She was not. I will go back to sleep, Gerald North thought, and wake up again and start it all over — start it in a room which is not strange, with a wife where she ought to be, and certainly with no announcement about pelicans. Pelicans, for the love of God! What are pelicans to me or I to . . .

There was, he began to realize, something in his subconscious. It squirmed; it was rather like a tickle. It was not a pelican; too small for that. But it was, on the other hand, *not* not a pelican. A dream about a pelican? About, perhaps, a pelican who had carried away Pamela North? He leafed over such dreams as he could lay his mind on. If Pam had been carried away by anything, look under

"Nightmares." If . . .

Gerald North's subconscious said the hell with it, and opened enough to be peeked into. Its interior was dim, foggy. But there was something moving in it. For some seconds, what was moving kept slipping back into the fog. But then . . .

It was Pam moving, lightly, quickly. It was Pam putting on shorts and a pull-over shirt. He was —

"Go back to sleep," Pam said, in the fog of a dream which was not quite right for a dream. "It's early yet. I'm going out to fish for pelicans."

Jerry North sat on the side of his bed and ran the fingers of both hands through his hair. That was it, all right. Pam had got up and partly awakened him and said she was going out to fish for pelicans. Jerry had a momentary wish he had left that bit in his subconscious where, if anywhere, it belonged. Had he then told Pam a fact about pelicans and, contented at having set her straight, gone back to sleep? Or had he, himself sleepily satisfied, said only, "Mmmm," or some such thing, before he was asleep again? He was inclined to think the latter. A few words would have saved Pam from disappointment, and he had not spoken the words. Somewhere — probably out on the pier — Pam was hopefully fishing for pelicans.

Jerry released his head and stood up, and finally did waken. He was in their room in The Coral Isles, city of Key West, state of Florida. That sharded brightness so painful to the eyes came from the Atlantic Ocean, with the morning sun on it. The time was eight-fifteen, the date the fourteenth of February, the temperature was already in the seventies. From the window of their room, Jerry could not see the fishing pier. He had better, he decided, dress and go find Pam and tell her she hadn't a prayer, because pelicans are birds.

The Coral Isles was barely half awake. In the lobby a man was pushing a vacuum cleaner back and forth; on the deep porch on the ocean side the chairs were in an orderly row, their backs to the wall. A man was sprinkling the crab grass. (No. Mustn't be impolite. The Bermuda grass.) At the far end of the two-hundred-foot pier there was a small figure.

Jerry took the path to the pier. Larry Saunders, the tennis pro, was dragging a heavy brush back and forth across the near court. He flicked a hand in greeting; he said it was going to be another warm one; he hoped it wasn't going to be so windy. Jerry went past the swimming pool. A very tanned young man in white trunks was cleaning it. Jerry went past the sunning enclosure in the lee of the bathhouse — and, according to the brochure, the solaria and the new and fully equipped gymnasium. Nobody was sunning yet.

He went out onto the long, narrow pier — a wooden structure on piles above the glittering water of the Atlantic. (Unless, by this time, the Atlantic had become the Gulf?) The crepe soles of his Keds made little sound on the planking.

It was Pam, all right. She was on the platform at the end of the pier — the stubby crossing of an elongated T. Her back was to him, and she was unquestionably fishing. And —

Jerry stopped in midstep. And — *she had caught pelicans!*

There was a pelican to the right of her on the platform, and a pelican to the left of her. They were large and motionless; crouching pelicans, with preposterous pouches under their bills.

Damn it all, Jerry thought. They *are* birds. You don't —

Pam pulled up her line. If she's caught another, Jerry thought, I'll — I'll — He put a hand on the nearer rail to steady himself.

A small bright object dangled at the end of Pam North's line. One of the pelicans got up, and extended its big wings, as if it were stretching. It waddled a step nearer Pam North.

Pam detached a small fish from the hook,

10

and turned to the pelican and said, "Here" and tossed. The little fish disappeared into the large pelican. The pelican moved back and sat down.

All right, Jerry North thought. Language is a clumsy thing, full of knobs. "For pelicans." All right. "For" pelicans if one liked. "In behalf of pelicans" would, certainly, have made things clearer — a little clearer. He went on, joined Pam.

"That Miss Brownley left yesterday," Pam said. "She's been fishing for them every morning. They're so trusting, the poor things."

Jerry looked from pelican to pelican.

"I can't," Jerry North said, "say they look it. Are they sick or something?"

One of the pelicans made a somewhat guttural noise at him. It was the one who had not got the last fish.

"Why sick?" Pam said. "I don't think they're sick. They have fine appetites. All *right*." The last was, Jerry gathered, to the more talkative of the pelicans. Pam dropped her line in again.

"Is there," Jerry said, "some reason they can't do their own fishing?"

"Probably forgotten how," Pam said. "Would you if you didn't have to?"

The pelican which had spoken stood up, stretched wings, and advanced two steps. It

11

had, Jerry thought, a definite let's-get-on-with-it attitude. "I know it's your turn," Pam said. "As soon as — " She pulled her line in sharply, and another bright fish twisted in the sunlight. Pam North said "Here," again, and tossed again.

"And," Pam said, "the soup kitchen is closing for the day." She reeled her line in and both pelicans watched her through red eyes. Then the pelican who had eaten last said something rather like "awrk" and made a small hop and extended wings and went off, looking like an old-fashioned flying boat. The other pelican watched and it occurred to Jerry its eyes had a bet-I-could-do-that expression. It looked at Pam. "No," Pam said. "Maybe tomorrow." The pelican flew away.

"I," Pamela North said, "smell like a fish."

They walked back along the pier, which extended north and south from sand to ocean, and over ocean. Jerry walked on Pam's left; at Key West the trade winds are easterly.

"A little," Jerry said. "Down here almost everything does. Are you going to adopt those pelicans?" He paused briefly. "Birds," he said. He still felt vaguely that that ought to be kept straight.

Pam has a tendency to extend protection to all creatures, whatever their plumage, the number of their legs, she feels may be in need of it. Jerry could, offhand, think of no special reasons why pelicans should be excluded.

"They look healthy enough to me," he added.

"Heavy flyers," Pam said. "As if they were too big for themselves. Of course, they do like early breakfasts." Pam yawned, and covered yawning. She looked at her hand reproachfully. "Very like a fish," she said. "I expect as I get adjusted."

One learns by experience, of which Gerald North has had considerable. Pamela's last remark was therefore, to him, entirely comprehensible. Of recent months, Pam had developed a habit of waking early. It was to be expected, and by Jerry greatly hoped, that the soft air of the South, the listlessness of vacation, would return her to more reasonable ways. If it did, the pelicans could awrk for their breakfasts. (As long, of course, as they remained in health.)

"Awrk," Jerry said, experimentally. It did not sound much like a pelican asking to be fed. Pam, reasonably enough, said, "Huh?"

"Worked with the pelicans," Jerry said. "Say 'awrk' and get your breakfast."

"It didn't sound like 'awrk' to me," Pam said. "But have it your own way. I'll have to shower and change first."

They reached the shore end of the pier and

Pam leaned her rod against the bathhouse. There was still no one in the sunning place. At the fresh-water pool, the tanned young man in white trunks was putting pads on wooden chaises. Larry Saunders was brushing the second tennis court. The man was still watering crab grass. Mr. Grogan stood at the head of the steps which led up to the porch of The Coral Isles. Mr. Grogan had the red face of a man who, by choice and profession, spends most of his time in the sun and who does not tan. He had snowy white hair; a wave of white hair crested from forehead to nape of neck.

"Beautiful morning," Mr. Grogan told the Norths. "Going to be a fine day. Probably get to eighty or thereabouts."

The managing director of a resort hotel is concerned with such matters, keeping one eye on the thermometer and the other on the guest roster.

"Been feeding Eddy and Freddy?" Mr. Grogan said.

Pam said, "Pelicans?"

"People call them Eddy and Freddy," Mr. Grogan said. "I've no idea why. Freddy and Frederica, for all I know. Don't even know if it's always the same two."

"Pelicans," Pam North said, "do look like pelicans."

14

"There's that, Mrs. North," Mr. Grogan said. "May be different ones every time. Anyway, there are always two when anybody fishes there. Freeloaders." He looked with approval out over the sparkling Atlantic, a desirable facility for any resort hotel. "Putting on weight, they are," he said. "Probably take it off in the summer, though."

This was winter. Here, it was hard to remember that. Driving the day before through the city of Key West they had slowed to ten, or thereabouts, in school zones, and Pam, speaking for them both, and speaking in wonderment, had said, "Schools open? This time of year?" and, after a momentary pause, "Oh. Of course."

This was not summer. This was February. In the summer, there would be none to feed pelicans. Pelicans would have to fend for themselves.

A youth in a red jacket came out of the lobby. Mr. Grogan was apparently still looking at the ocean. But, in some fashion, he saw the youth behind him. He said, "All right, Jimmy," and "Have a good day," to the Norths, and went back into the hotel, his crested hair a white sail in the easterlies.

"I won't be a minute," Pam said, when they were, themselves, inside. "You get a table."

Jerry got the Miami *Herald*. "NEW BLIZ-

15

ZARD SWEEPS NORTH," the streamer headline said. The day before, the headline had read: "ICY BLASTS BATTER NORTHLAND." Today's story, under a New York date line, began: "Three inches of snow covered New York City today in the wake of a coastal storm which brought winds of more than twenty miles an hour and subfreezing temperatures to the entire metropolitan area." A blizzard, Jerry thought, is in the eye of the beholder. Or, of course, the headline writer.

He sat in the lobby, reading the *Herald*. The world wagged as gloomily as ever, but for the most part on the second page. There had been a three-car smashup on Biscayne Boulevard. Somebody had managed to drive off the Sunshine Turnpike at an estimated ninety. The mysterious disappearance of "heiress" remained mysterious.

The alarm clock which ticks in proper husbands tinkled in Jerry's mind. Of Pam's minute, fifteen had elapsed. He went into the dining room and was led to a table by a window. He ordered orange juice, in honor of the state, and coffee, in pursuance of a mounting need. They, and Pam, arrived simultaneously. Pam was dressed for tennis. She carried mail.

There was a large brown envelope with "North Books, Inc.," and an address in the

16

upper left-hand corner. Jerry North sighed, the sigh of a man pursued. He put the envelope in his pocket. There was a letter with "Mrs. William Weigand" and an address printed on the flap. Dorian Weigand wrote in envy. Bill Weigand wrote a postscript: "Murders routine. Regards cordial."

"So we'll know we're not missing anything," Pam said. "Nice of Bill."

"Dull days at Homicide West," Jerry said, and knew that the days there were never really dull; that Captain William Weigand was not finding that time hung heavy. Homicide is endemic in Manhattan, West Side or East. It was pleasant to think that here, as far south as one could get in the United States, only fish would die by violence — fish, and of course motorists.

They finished breakfast. The New York *Times* and the *Herald Tribune* had not arrived. "Terrible weather up there," the girl at the newsstand said, happily. "I understand all the planes are grounded." On the porch they divided the Miami *Herald*, which is susceptible to almost infinite subdivision. People in bathing suits walked in front of them. Most of the women carried enormous bags, and most of these were made of brightly colored straw. The men wore straw hats of peculiar shapes and colors or, for variety, yachting caps. The man who had been watering crab grass had changed his hose for a power mower, which smoked furiously. A young man and a girl walked, hand in hand, up the slight slope to the swimming pool and, still hand in hand, dived in. A small boy with a tennis racket walked by, bound for a lesson.

"We've got a date at ten-thirty with that nice doctor and Rebecca somebody," Pam said. Jerry pushed aside a light film of sleep and said he hadn't forgotten. At a quarter after ten he said, no, he still hadn't forgotten, and went up to their room to change. As was inevitable, the maid was in the room. She accepted intrusion with tight-lipped politeness and went with the air of one who would try, but not desperately, to come back and finish up.

Pam was sitting under the awning at the tennis courts, beside a tall, spare man. As Jerry came up she said, "Called Teddy and Freddy for some reason. Here he is now."

The spare man turned in his chair and then stood up, and Jerry said, "Morning, doctor," to Dr. Edmund Piersal who said, "Good morning, Mr. North. Not so much wind today."

The day before, when they had first met at the courts, looked at each other appraisingly, in the manner of tennis players, and agreed to hit a few, it had been windy. High hedges of evergreens beyond the wire netting

18

around the courts gave some shelter. It was still windy. And Dr. Piersal had been too good, but not too overwhelmingly too good. (6–3.) Piersal had said, "Off your game, I imagine," and Jerry had not too openly accepted this judgment, but had not entirely rejected it. "Haven't played since September," was his nonrejection. "Not that you wouldn't take me any time."

Which had been true yesterday, and probably would be today. Piersal was several inches over six feet, which is no disadvantage in tennis; he was lean and tanned. He was also, at Jerry's guess, in his early sixties. There was more gray than black in his thick hair; there were deep lines in his thin, firm face. ("A man of distinction, except he looks too bright for it," Pam had said, when they reviewed the previous day over cocktails.) Dr. Piersal also had a good backhand.

Jerry sat down; already the shade was pleasant. (Mr. Grogan, specialist in resort hotels, was also pretty good about the weather.)

"She ought to be along soon," Dr. Piersal said. He had a quiet voice. "No idea what sort of game she plays."

Pickup tennis at a resort hotel is hit or miss. The day before, Rebecca something — Jerry groped; Rebecca Payne — had merely sat and watched, although she had been dressed for tennis. She had watched through black eyes, set deeply in a thinnish face; she had watched, Jerry thought, wistfully. Such other women as came to the courts came paired. After some time of watching, she had tucked her racket under her arm and gone away, walking quickly and well and as if she were going some place. (I'm afraid she isn't, really, Pam North had thought.)

It was Dr. Piersal who had set up the mixed doubles for which, sitting in the awning shade, they now waited. "Ran into that dark girl," he had said the afternoon before, running into Jerry in the lobby. "All by herself, apparently. You and your wife like to take us on tomorrow?"

They watched a small boy taking a tennis lesson on the far court. Larry Saunders was tall and patient in mid-court, with a big basket, half full of gray tennis balls, at his feet. "Stay away from it, Jamie," Saunders said, and bounced another ball to forehand. "That's better."

Jamie hit the ball over the backstop. "Not quite so hard, Jamie," Saunders said. "Take your time." He bounced another ball. Jamie hit it; Jerry reached in front of Pam and caught it, and threw it back. Both courts were littered with gray tennis balls. "Move up on it if you have to, Jamie," Saunders said. "That a boy." Jamie hit a ball toward the curiously shaped building which was, Jerry had found out the day before, an outsize cistern. It dated back to the days when Key West lived by water which dripped from roofs. The Navy fed its thirst now, by pipeline from distant Homestead.

"I'm so sorry," Rebecca Payne said. "Zipper." She indicated the zipper on her white shorts. "I brought some balls," she said, a little hurriedly. She took off a blue jacket and began to twist the ribbon of metal from the top of a can of tennis balls. "I'm afraid I'm not any good," she said. "I'll spoil your game, probably. But the doctor said — "

"You can't," Pam said, "be worse than I am."

This proved inaccurate. Rebecca Payne was slim and quick, and she had had lessons. But she was obviously very tense, very — "embarrassed" is the word, Pam thought, and hit a wicked drop shot for Dr. Piersal's consideration. It was touch and go. "Not up, I'm afraid," Dr. Piersal said, gasping slightly.

A good many men would, under the circumstances, hog the court, Pam thought. All tennis players prefer to win, and that is the way for Piersal and Rebecca Payne to win. And it would have been a way to tell Rebecca Payne what, too evidently, she already knew — that, on a tennis court, she was not to be

21

trusted; that here she could not, really, stand on her own two feet. It would have been a way to humiliate her.

A nice man, Pam thought. A really nice man. She gave the nice man another drop shot to try for. "You are," Dr. Piersal said, with apparent delight, "an evil woman." He said, "I'm sorry, partner," to Rebecca, who shook her head and flushed deeply. She knocked one of the gray balls back onto the lesson court.

She served the last game, the last brief game. One does not return service within reach of as tall and lithe a net man as Dr. Edmund Piersal had proved to be — all instincts, including that of self-preservation, are against it. Pam and Jerry returned to Rebecca Payne, making bounces as honest as they could manage, playing to the forehand. One of Jerry's returns floated within reach of Piersal, and that, although not in a manner to endanger either North, was that, and brought the score to fifteen–forty. It had gone on long enough, Pam thought, and drove to the dark girl's alley.

"We need a drink," Piersal said, in the awning's shade. "I prescribe — "

"I'm sorry," Rebecca said, and her voice was tense. "I spoiled your game — everybody's game."

And then, slender, erect — and beaten —

she walked away.

"She hurts herself," Pam said. "And — it's all about nothing. Who cares about a game of tennis?"

"She does," Piersal said. "About everything, probably. About the drink — "

But then, although he was still some thirty feet away, Mr. Grogan said, "Oh, Edmund. Spare me a moment?" He stopped and waited for Dr. Piersal to come to him and that, Pam thought, was unlike Paul Grogan. She had met Grogan less than forty-eight hours before but she was still quite sure that waiting to be walked to was unlike him.

The two men spoke briefly. Then Piersal turned and said, across the space, "Sorry. A rain check?"

"Of course," Jerry said.

Then the tall doctor and Paul Grogan walked away together. They walked, Pam thought, rather quickly.

II

Pam and Jerry played a set. Jerry ran, pantingly, for drop shots. Pam waved, admiringly, at drives. "You don't run," Jerry said. "That's what it is."

"I run this way," Pam said; "they go that way."

"And there's the matter of your feet," Jerry said.

"I know all about my feet."

Jerry served and Pam's drop shot seemed to climb wearily over the net. The effort exhausted it. It died on clay. He served again; was drop-shotted again.

"There's the matter of your own feet," Pam told him, with affection.

Jerry won, as was customary; at six–two, which was also customary. He felt as if he had been running uphill for a long time. They sat again under the awning, damp, contented. Pam said, "For heaven's sake. He's wearing clothes." Jerry looked.

The man approaching had narrow shoulders and a narrow face, and he was, unmistakably, wearing clothes. He was wearing a dark business suit; his shirt was complete with tie. He even wore a hat. It occurred to Jerry that there was not, in all Key West, another man so attired. He came toward them and said, to two white-clad humans, both of them dripping moderately, "Been having a game?"

"Yes," Jerry said. "Tennis."

The man in the business suit saw nothing odd about this answer. Jerry felt he had wasted it.

"Name of Ashley," the man said.

"North."

The man who had the name of Ashley looked away abruptly; looked toward the swimming pool.

"I'll swear it is," Ashley said. "What do you know?"

The Norths looked toward the swimming pool. A man was coming down from it, along the path toward the courts. He, also, wore a business suit. He wore a Panama hat. He, too, was a narrow man.

Ashley looked at Pam North, at Jerry North. He said, in a tone of awe, "Worthington."

"I'm sorry," Jerry said. "We're both sorry," Pam said, feeling that two could play at this game, also.

"Down from Hialeah," Ashley said. "What do you know?"

"I'm afraid — " Jerry North said.

"*Must* have heard of him," Ashley said.

"Everybody's heard of him. Worthington Farms. Kentucky."

"I'm sorry," Pam North said.

The man under the Panama advanced toward them.

"Thoroughbreds," Ashley said. "Derby winner. Triple crown."

"Oh," Pam said, "you mean he raises horses?"

Ashley looked at her quickly. He looked away again. He raised his voice slightly. He said, "Mr. Worthington?"

The man under the Panama said, "Yup."

"Name of Ashley. Met you at — "

"Yup. 'Lo, Ashley."

"Mr. North. Mrs. North."

The man under the Panama said, "Ma'am. Sir."

"Down from Hialeah?"

"Yup."

"I wonder if — " Ashley said.

"Thought you might," Worthington said. "Yup. Ladybug in the sixth. Monday. Shoo-in. Short odds. Maybe three to one. Can't have everything. Five lengths, could be. Well, got a plane to catch. Ma'am. Sir. Ashley."

He turned, as if to go away. He did not, Pam thought, turn with any decisiveness.

Ashley looked at Jerry North and raised his eyebrows. Jerry was conscious that he himself blinked slightly.

"If you're going back to Miami," Ashley said, to Worthington, who did not, Pam thought, actually seem to be going any place. "On this filly. I can't get away. Stuck here. Wonder if — "

"You'll talk about it. Gets out and the odds — "

"Mum," Ashley said. "As an oyster, Mr. Worthington. It would be a favor. Isn't often anybody can get the word from a man like you, Mr. Worthington. Is it, Mr. North?"

There was excitement in Ashley's voice. There was even a kind of awe in his voice. Opportunity, his tone said, was not only knocking at the door. It was trying to beat the door down.

"I guess not," Jerry said. There was, somewhere, a light tapping.

"Not much," Ashley said, again to Worthington. "Not enough to hurt the odds. Maybe fifty?"

He reached to his hip pocket, took a wallet out. "If I can feel I've got my own money on her — "

"You'll keep your mouth shut," Worthington said. "Generous of you, suh."

Ashley waited. Worthington considered; his narrow face was all consideration.

"Sort of got me, haven't you?" he said.

27

"Well — all right."

"My friend here, too?"

Ashley indicated Gerald North.

Mr. Worthington sighed heavily, a man trapped by his own inadvertence.

"You're crowding me," he said. "But — yup." He took a small notebook from his pocket. It had a pencil between the leaves.

"Thomas J. Ashley," Ashley said. "I'm staying at the Key Lodge."

"Fifty on the nose," Worthington said. He sighed again. Ashley opened his wallet and gave Worthington a bill. It was a fifty-dollar bill. Worthington looked at Jerry. Jerry felt, momentarily and obscurely, that this had all been decided.

"Gerald — " he began, and Mr. Worthington began to write in his small notebook. And Jerry was aware that his hand was reaching toward Pam's straw handbag, in which, when they are dressed for tennis, all things are carried, including billfolds.

But then Ashley, who was looking toward the hotel, made a small "uh-uhing" sound, and the man named Worthington looked in the same direction, and Pam and Jerry looked.

Paul Grogan, managing director of The Coral Isles, was advancing, under the white plume of his hair — a plume which had become a banner. While he was still many yards

28

away, Mr. Grogan held his right hand out stiffly, the index finger pointing like a gun.

Mr. Worthington did not say anything at all. He began to walk briskly toward the patio, beyond which there was an exit to the street. Mr. Ashley said, "Well . . ." and also went.

"And stay out," Mr. Grogan said, still from a distance, and in what was not quite a shout. "Catch you here once more and . . ."

He did not finish. It was evident that he was not going to catch the Messrs. Worthington and Ashley. Not without running. He did not run. He walked on, still briskly, to the Norths. He said, "That pair of small-time con men. I hope you didn't fall for — "

"Of course not," Pam North said. "We never even thought of it, did we, Jerry?"

Jerry swallowed. Jerry said, "Of course not."

"Ashley," Grogan said. "Not that his name is Ashley, probably. Anyway, he's been at it for years, with one partner and another. Other one's new. Heard somewhere he used to be a lawyer in New York and got in some kind of a jam. Got in jail too, apparently. Anyway — " He shrugged his shoulders, and responsibility for two small-time con men slipped from them.

"Hope I didn't break up your game," Grogan said. "Dragging Dr. Piersal away like

29

that. Dr. Townsend — he's the house physician, you know — is under the — " Grogan interrupted himself. One does not, operating a hotel in Key West, speak disparagingly of the weather. "Laid up," he said. "One of the guests came down with something — something minor, I'm sure — and I asked Edmund to look in on her. His line of country and — " Again he stopped.

"What," Pam asked, "is Dr. Piersal's line of country?"

"Internist," Grogan said. "Pretty well-known New York man. He's — "

"Wait a minute," Jerry said. "I have heard of him. Isn't he a man who gets called in at murder trials? Expert on forensic medicine? Wait a minute. Wasn't he a deputy medical examiner of New York City for a while? Wasn't he — "

"Lectures on forensic medicine at Dyckman University," Grogan said. "Yes, that's the man. Primarily an internist, but the other things too. The point is — "

"You didn't break up the game," Pam said. "We'd lost our fourth already. Rebecca Payne. She — there was something else she had to do."

Paul Grogan nodded his head.

"I hope there was," he said. "I really do. I'm afraid the girl isn't having a very good time, y'know. We've got so few singles at

30

the moment. Never very many any time, of course, but just now — "

A young man in a red coat appeared on the steps which led down from the wide porch. He looked around. Paul Grogan had his back to the hotel.

"I'm wanted for something, apparently," he said. "Lunch in the patio today, with the wind down." Paul Grogan faced the Atlantic. He took two deep breaths. He went away toward the hotel.

Jerry gazed after him. He did this for some seconds. After Mr. Grogan had reached the hotel and gone into it, Jerry continued to look in the direction.

"All right," Pam said; "grant he has got them."

Jerry returned, not rapidly. He said, "Huh?"

"Eyes in the back of," Pam said. "Probably standard equipment for hotel managers. Or maybe it's like dogs."

Jerry returned his attention entirely to his wife. "Huh?" seemed somewhat inadequate, but he used it.

"Invisible whistles," Pam said. "I mean inaudible, of course. The bellmen carry them and Mr. Grogan tunes in and — where *had* you gone, Jerry?"

"Something rang a bell," Jerry said. "About

31

Dr. Piersal. It was in the papers. Last fall sometime."

Pam North lifted her shoulders, disclaiming knowledge. She is a selective reader of newspapers — crosswords and bridge columns; book and play reviews; James Reston and Walter Lippmann. And stories about children the world has made unhappy. Having disclaimed with her shoulders, she shook her head.

"Malpractice suit," Jerry said. "I don't remember the details. Surviving relative of a non-surviving patient. The Damocles sword over all physicians. Malice and cupidity and — " He shrugged.

"And sometimes, I suppose, malpractice," Pam said.

It had not been, this time, Jerry told her. Newspapers generally play down such suits. This one had been rather special, partly because of Dr. Piersal's standing; partly because the jury had found for him after ten minutes' consideration; largely because of the remarks of Supreme Court Justice Bleeker, who had commended the jury for its wisdom, and gone further. Justice Bleeker was notably peppery, and inclined to have his say.

He had had it this time at length. Jerry did not remember the details, but the burden had been scathing. This suit against a man of Dr.

Piersal's standing, his acknowledged distinction in his field, his record of unselfish service to — in any event, this suit had been a flagrant example of the unjustified harassment to which physicians are too much subject. It was hard for Justice Bleeker to believe that plaintiff's lawyer had not recognized this. It was hard for Justice Bleeker to believe that a desire to besmirch had not been linked, in this instance, with the desire for gain. In fewer words, Justice Bleeker took a dim view.

And this had made the papers, as the remarks of Supreme Court Justice Bleeker frequently did.

"Anybody can tell Dr. Piersal's a good doctor," Pam said, after Jerry's resumé. "Just by looking at him."

Jerry looked at Pam.

"He was so nice to poor Miss Payne," Pam said. "We'd better change, hadn't we? Unless you want another?"

"Had enough for the second day," Jerry said.

They walked to their room and showered, Pam for the second time within a few hours, with the expressed hope that she did not prove soluble. Jerry's change was to walking shorts and polo shirt; Pam's to a greenish print dress. They went to sit on stools at the outdoor bar near the swimming pool, and at

33

first they were alone.

"They don't drink much here, do they?" Pam said. "The poor dears. Just sit and swelter. And turn those odd colors, of course."

Slowly, they sipped long drinks. Idly, they watched young men in white jackets and women — not so uniformly young — setting up tables in the patio. "There's the doctor," Pam said, after some time, and nodded a directing head. Dr. Edmund Piersal was standing near the tennis courts, looking around. Pam held a hand up and closed fingers, beckoning. Piersal waved, and started toward them.

He wore slacks and a dark blue polo shirt and a white jacket. He sat on the other side of Pam. He said, "Sorry, occupational hazard. Paul asked — "

"He told us," Pam said, and Dr. Piersal nodded his head and said, "Gin and tonic," to the barman, and waggled a thumb at the North glasses and said, "When they're ready."

Pam hoped it had not been anything serious.

"Tummy ache," Piersal said. "Sort of thing that worries Paul, of course. Wanted me to find out if she ate here last night. I don't mean that was his primary concern but — " He shrugged wide shoulders.

"Did she?" Pam said.

Piersal laughed briefly. He said she hadn't.

He said that had been a relief to Paul Grogan.

"Anyway," he said, "according to her version of her history, it's functional. 'Nervous indigestion.' Doesn't mean a damn thing, of course. The term doesn't. Useful, because a good many people have it. 'Present-day tensions,' as the television medicine men say. They tell me you're a book publisher, Mr. North."

They turned from medicine, as it was evident Dr. Piersal wished to turn. A patient, Pam decided, is a patient, even if anonymous, and so not to be discussed. Jerry admitted he published books. He admitted it a little glumly; it was not, that day, a subject which enlivened his spirits. Book-of-the-Month had, after what Jerry considered a good deal of hemming and hawing, decided against "Away Again." Lester Spears, whose option had run out, had been seen lunching with Bingham, of Bingham, Foster, Kelly and Breckenridge, and Spears's last had made the list. An author into which North Books had been patiently poking advances, in the dimming hope of a jackpot, no longer answered letters. Yet continued to endorse checks.

Pam said, after a time, "You must get in quite a bit of tennis, Dr. Piersal."

Dr. Piersal did get in quite a bit of tennis. There was a club — call it a club — near

Hawthorne which owned two excellent clay courts, housed for winter. Piersal got up a couple of times a week. Nobody too good, nobody too bad. "You'd both fit in fine," Piersal said.

They talked of tennis, as tennis players must. They sipped long drinks, and the sun was warm on their backs, but the easterly tempered it. Dr. Piersal recommended, mildly, the greyhound races at Stock Island. He had been there the night before. Men in chef's caps began to carry platters to the buffet table; a large fan at one end of the table began to blow flies away. From the sunning beach, men and women began to trickle; a small turbulence formed at one end of the buffet table.

Jerry finished his drink; Jerry said, "Well — " Dr. Piersal said, "Let me. I suggested it," and signed the check. It did not matter. There would be another day; tomorrow would be another day; a week from tomorrow would be still another. "Think about this Hawthorne place," Piersal said, and stood up. "We certainly will," Pam said. There was a place for lunch near the Aquarium, Piersal told them. The broiled shrimps with white wine sauce were excellent. "Perhaps tomorrow," Jerry said. It would be hot on Duval Street; cars would be creeping on Duval Street in the day's heat. The trade winds seem to die in Duval Street.

They watched Dr. Edmund Piersal, a tall, lithe man who walked like a man of thirty, as he went toward the hotel — went to walk through it, toward car or taxi; toward, in the end, shrimps broiled in white wine sauce.

"A nice man," Pam said.

"Very."

"This place in Hawthorne sounds interesting. I suppose we ought to."

"It sounds interesting."

"But we won't, will we?"

"I don't suppose we will, Pam."

"We're stick-in-the-muds, aren't we?"

"It's pleasant mud."

The thing to do with a buffet is to walk around it first, to case it. Otherwise one may come too late on the especially succulent, come with plate already piled high. It is well to stake a table, preferably one under an umbrella. The Norths found a shaded table; put tennis rackets and a can of balls on it, marking their homestead rights. "You'll never eat all that," Pam said, and a waitress brought them iced coffee. Pam was wrong. "My," Pam said, "you're not like that at home."

The New York *Times* had come. The *Herald Tribune* had come. Blizzards had been defied. "All main city thoroughfares are reported clear," the *Herald Tribune* assured them. The *Times,* on page 94 referred, with marked de-

tachment, to "yesterday's light snowfall."
Jerry dozed; dreamed briefly of pelicans.

"Fresh or salt?" Pam said, after she had finished the *Times* crossword.

The pelicans flew, sluggishly, from Jerry's dreams.

They left the porch, changed to swim. They went halfway out on the fishing pier, and down a flight of wooden steps to a bit of the Atlantic which lived in a cage of netting. "To discourage barracuda," Jerry had said the day before, and had discouraged Pam, so that they dunked in the fresh-water pool. But Mr. Grogan, after dinner, had laughed at that — laughed, Jerry thought, a little excessively.

They floated in salt water, now and then swishing mildly. Small fish, conceivably infant barracuda, swam with them. Very tiny fish swam in a formation of hundreds. Pam splashed a hand and the fish, formation still impeccable, turned aside. "They must drill and drill," Pam said. "Like cadets." They could look under the pier, set on piles above the water. Thin edges of light worked between planks, made bright, straight ribbons on the water. Above them, on the pier, people walked back and forth. Beyond the netting, gulls sat on water, bobbing gently, making an occasional strident remark.

The Norths went back to their room, and

showered again — "Do they have to use this much chlorine?" "The Navy is our first line of defense" — and mildly debated more tennis, but were interrupted by sleep. They went to the Penguin Bar and had a drink. They went to a place, built out over water, called the A. & B. Lobster House, and, not sharing native belief that Florida "lobsters" are edible, had pompano. They went back to the hotel and, briefly, danced in the patio.

"A day of accomplishment," Jerry said, as they walked down the second-floor corridor to their room. "A night's repose well earned."

"They've turned down the beds," Pam said. "I think we ought to live this way all the time."

III

It was not, this time, the sound of his own voice that wakened Gerald North. It was his own name. It was "Jerry! *Jerry!*" Hands were on his shoulders, shaking him awake. "Wake up," Pam was saying. "Please — *please* — wake up! *Jerry.*"

Jerry was awake. Wakening was a plunge from warmth into icy water.

Pam was leaning over him, her hands on his shoulders.

Her face, so near his, was wrenched. Color had gone out of her face. "Wake up," she said once more and then he swung up, carrying her with him, and she held to him. She was trembling; her body shook.

"On the pier," Pam said. "He's — shot. I don't know. Stabbed. There's — " He could feel her body steady, could feel a deep breath going into her lungs. "There's blood all over," she said. But her voice still shook. "Dr. Piersal. He's been killed. Somebody's killed him and — "

Again her body began to shake in his arms. He tightened his arms.

"I'll be all right," Pam said. "We've got — "

Jerry released her. In seconds he was in

shorts, in canvas shoes.

This morning — this still early morning — there was nobody in the lobby, no drone of vacuum. This morning the whole hotel seemed to sleep. "Sunday," Jerry thought, his mind flicking the word. This morning no man watered the lawns of The Coral Isles. As they ran toward the pier, they ran through a sleeping world. The gulls screamed harshly above them. A pelican sat on a pile, far out, and stared at them.

Edmund Piersal lay face down on the platform at the end of the pier. He wore walking shorts and a tennis shirt which had been white, and a gray sweater. Blood spread out from his body, but most of it had dripped between the planks, gone drop by drop into the water below.

He was, Jerry realized, done with bleeding. He was dead, now.

He lay on the wound which had killed him — the wound of knife or bullet, the wound through which his blood had flowed over boards, into water. He had not been dead long, Jerry guessed, but knew the roughness of a layman's guess.

He crouched beside Piersal's body. He stood up. "I'll go — " he began, and looked at Pam. She was standing very still; she was looking away, looking at the pelican on its post. Under

41

the faint flush of beginning sunburn her face was very white. He spoke her name, but she did not turn. She nodded her head, but did not turn.

"Go tell somebody," he said. "There'll be somebody at the desk. I'll stay here."

She nodded her head again. She said, "All right, Jerry," in a strange voice. Then she moved away. She took two quick steps. Then she began to run.

There was no hurry. Piersal would wait, would wait patiently for all the time there was. But there are conventions in such matters. Jerry North leaned against the rail and waited with him. Don't touch. See that the body isn't moved. Leave things as you find them; see that things are left.

"Don't tell me you left the body," Bill Weigand — Captain William Weigand — would say. "You ought to know better by now, Jerry."

Bill wasn't there. It was no business of Bill Weigand's. It is no business of mine, Jerry thought. No business of ours — just that lousy luck of ours. You find a body in a bathtub,* and your life is changed. Changed for keeps. It's going to be another hot day. We won't play tennis today. He had a hell of a good

* The Norths Meet Murder (1940).

42

backhand, Piersal had. He loved the game. Probably he loved many things — the feel of a ball hit cleanly, the taste of broiled shrimps in white wine sauce. All sorts of things. Big things and little things. Pam had told him about the pelicans and he had come out to see the pelicans and . . .

Jerry shivered slightly. Policemen are not fools. William Weigand of Homicide West was one of the most intelligent men Jerry knew. There is no implication of guilt in the finding of a man murdered. Forty-eight hours ago, neither he nor Pam had laid eyes on Dr. Edmund Piersal. Pam had not invited Edmund Piersal to pier's end to watch the feeding of pelicans. Of course she hadn't. Oh, she might have said, "You ought to see them, doctor. Funny birds. They think people were made to fish for pelicans."

Jerry looked, with something like anger, at the pelican on its post. Silly-looking damn bird. Teddy or Freddy or whatever.

There was movement at the shore end of the pier. A bellman in a red jacket ran along a path toward the pier. There wasn't really any hurry, Jerry thought. An hour or so ago there might have been a time for that. Behind the bellman, trotting, was Paul Grogan, with the morning sun on his white hair. He looked behind Grogan. There was nobody else. That was a good thing. Pam had seen enough for that day.

The bellman wore hard shoes. His feet thudded on the pier planking. He ran easily, as youth runs. Fifty feet or so away he suddenly stopped running, and came on slowly, with an odd kind of solemnity in his movement. He stopped some feet from the planks which were stained with blood. He said, "Jeeze." Color went out from under the tan on his face. He said, "He's dead, isn't he?"

"Yes," Jerry said. "He's dead."

Paul Grogan came up, his face redder than ever from his running. He looked at the body. He said, "My God. *Edmund.*" He looked at Jerry North.

"Yes," Jerry said. "He's dead."

Jerry felt a little, and unpleasantly, like a master of ceremonies.

He said, "You called the police?"

"County sheriff," Grogan said. "Who'd do a thing like this? To a man like Edmund Piersal?"

Jerry did not have the answers. He said, "You knew him pretty well?"

"Pretty well," Grogan said. "One of my regulars." Jerry raised his eyebrows slightly. It was as good a thing as any to talk about.

"People in my line," Grogan said. "People who manage resort hotels. Down here this time of year. Some place up north in the summers. This place one year, maybe another place another year. People get used to us. Figure it's the way a place is run as much as anything. A personal following. One of the things we have to sell. Four–five years ago, I managed a place up the Keys. Met the doctor then. Next summer, or maybe the summer after, it was a place in New Hampshire. He came there. Since then — " He shrugged.

"Alone?"

"The first time his wife was with him. She died. Alone since then. He was dead when your wife found him?"

"Yes," Jerry said.

"What do you suppose he was doing out here? He didn't fish much."

"I don't know," Jerry said.

Distantly, there was the sound of a siren.

"There they come," Grogan said. "A hell of a thing to happen."

This time, Jerry felt, he did not speak only of the hellish thing which had happened. Hotel managers prefer murders to occur, if they must at all, off the premises.

"Get out of here!" Grogan shouted, suddenly, and unexpectedly, at the pelican. His voice was angry. When a man is filled with anger, a man has to put it some place.

The pelican paid no attention.

"Stay here, Jimmy," Grogan said. "If you see anybody starting out — any of the guests, I mean — tell them . . ." He paused. "Tell them the pier isn't safe."

The bellman said, "Yes, sir." There was something wrong with his voice.

Grogan started to walk back along the pier, and Jerry went with him. When Grogan had walked twenty feet or so, he turned.

"Oh, Jimmy," he said. "Don't make it sound too permanent, huh? Tell them we'll have the pier fixed in — oh, a couple of hours."

Jimmy said, "Yes, sir."

Pam was sitting in a corner of a sofa in the hotel lobby. The sofa was much too large for her. She was sitting as straight as one may on a deep sofa; her hands were clasped in her lap. Jerry went over and sat beside her.

"I told him about the pelicans," Pam said. "Do you suppose he — he went to watch them? And that that was — "

"No," Jerry said. "I don't, Pam."

"That, if I hadn't told him — "

"No." He put an arm around her shoulders. "No."

The sirens came closer. They came up the drive from Flagler Avenue, and to the circle in front of The Coral Isles. The first one stopped, but another continued. They were, Jerry thought, policemen in love with the sound of their own sirens.

Two state troopers came in, revolvers heavy at their sides; their expressions those of men ready for anything, and rather expecting riots. They stood inside and looked around the lobby, the right hand of each close to a holstered gun.

"My," Pam North said, "what fierce policemen. You'd think somebody'd passed a stop sign."

Jerry was relieved. The implacable troopers had changed the subject.

The second siren stopped its wailing. After a few seconds a tall and youngish man, wearing a blue suit, came in and looked around the lobby. He was very tanned; he had light hair in sharp contrast to the mahogany of his face. He went to the desk. Paul Grogan had been behind the desk; now he came around it and joined the man in the blue suit and walked with him to where the Norths waited.

"This is Deputy Sheriff Jefferson," Grogan said. "This is Mr. and Mrs. North, sheriff."

"Deputy," Jefferson said. "Mr. North. Ma'am."

He turned. Two other men, also in civilian clothes, had come through the entrance. One of them had a camera. Deputy Sheriff Jefferson nodded at them, and indicated with his head the direction they were to take. He turned back to the Norths.

"Like to talk to you after a bit," he said. "Have a look-see first. All right?"

"We don't — " Jerry North said.

"Sure you don't," Jefferson said. "All the same. Won't be long."

"We," Pam said, "aren't going anywhere, sheriff."

Then he went across the lobby, and out onto the porch beyond it.

"I'd so hoped," Pam North said, "that we'd never find another body."

Grogan had gone back behind the desk. Now he came from behind it and went to the two state policemen who still stood, ready for anything, just inside the main entrance. He spoke to them. The Norths could not hear his words, but could guess. "They make it look as if the joint was raided," Jerry said. The policemen looked at each other; one of them shrugged. It was the shrug of a man who humors the not particularly rational. The two policemen went out. The Norths could hear their cars start up.

They waited. The young woman who ran the newsstand came in, and behind her a bellman carrying newspapers in a bundle. She opened the newsstand. A plump man and a plump woman came the length of the lobby, wearing bright clothing, bound for breakfast.

Grogan said, "Good morning, Mr. Umph. Mrs. Umph. Looks like another beautiful day." Mr. Umph said "umph," or something like it. A tall young man and a pretty girl walked through the lobby hand in hand. A little girl of about three, in a bright yellow dress, ran through the lobby, screaming. Her screams were happy screams. From the far end of the lobby a man called, *"Margie!"* If the little girl was Margie she chose not to be reminded of it. A waiter went through the lobby, wheeling a breakfast cart. The Coral Isles was beginning to stretch itself awake.

Deputy Sheriff Jefferson came in from the porch side and spoke first to Paul Grogan, who was standing near the desk. Grogan nodded his head. Jefferson came to the Norths. He pulled a chair up and sat in front of them.

"Now, ma'am," Jefferson said. "About when was it?"

"About," Pam said. She looked at the clock over the fireplace — the fireplace which showed no sign of any use. "About forty-five minutes ago."

Jefferson looked at the clock.

"About seven-fifteen," he said. "That about right?"

"Yes."

"By yourself, Mrs. North?"

"Yes."

"Do you mind telling me why, Mrs. North?"

Jerry could feel it coming. It came. He noticed, not without sympathy, the expression in the eyes of the deeply tanned, youngish deputy sheriff.

"That is," Jerry said, "to catch fish for the pelicans. People do, you know."

Jefferson looked at him.

"They expect it," Pam said. "Mr. Grogan says they're called Teddy and Freddy. And I always get up early anyway."

Jefferson looked at Mrs. North. He took a deep breath. His wide chest swelled with it.

"Yes, ma'am," he said. "I see. You went out to fish for — to catch fish for pelicans. You found Dr. Piersal. You thought he was dead?"

"Yes," Pam North said. "I was quite sure he was dead. You can almost always tell. And there was so much . . ." She did not finish that. Jerry could see her pale again under the beginning sunburn.

"A lady like you," Jefferson said. "I shouldn't think — well, ma'am, it sounded as if you had — " He paused, clearly seeking words. "Had experience," he said, "coming up with them. With — that is, with dead bodies."

"Oh, yes," Pam said. "Quite a little, sheriff. Since the one in the bathtub."

50

It was true, of course. Pamela North is a truthful person. And she had, of course, been asked. She might, Jerry thought, have left out the bathtub bit. She had, he realized, put it in for clarification.

"Bathtub?" Jefferson said. "What's about a bathtub?"

"It was a long time ago," Jerry said, rather hurriedly. "It hasn't anything to do with this."

"Of course not," Pam said. "That one was named Brent. And he was a lawyer, not a doctor."

It had all come about naturally, Jerry thought. One thing had led to another. For some reason, one thing always did. Particularly, of course, with Pam.

"Sheriff," Gerald North said firmly, "several years ago we found the body of a murdered man in a bathtub. As a result of that we met a detective — a New York City detective. Captain William Weigand, a homicide man. As a result of meeting him we've been — " He checked himself. The words "mixed up in several murders" would not, he thought, be well-chosen words. "Interested in some of his cases," Jerry said.

Deputy Sheriff Jefferson appeared to consider this. Then he said, "Oh." Then he said, "I guess that explains it." He did not speak with assurance. He said, "Let's get back to

51

Dr. Piersal, ma'am."

Pam said, "Let's."

"You didn't expect to find him there?" Jefferson asked her.

"Of course not."

"I meant," Jefferson said, "find him alive?"

"If you think I went out there to meet him, I didn't. Why — that is, I certainly didn't. We hardly knew him at all."

"Sheriff," Jerry said, "we met him for the first time day before yesterday. Played tennis with him yesterday. Had a drink with him before lunch."

"He comes from New York," Jefferson said. "Came. You're New Yorkers, aren't you?"

Both Norths nodded their heads.

"You didn't know him there?"

Jerry said, "No."

Pam said, "There are millions of people in New York."

"You'd heard of him? Mr. Grogan says he was a very well-known man."

"I'd heard his name," Jerry said. "I realized that after we met him here."

"You came down here to fish, I suppose?"

"I don't — " Jerry said.

"Most people come to the Keys to fish," Jefferson said.

"We," Jerry said, "came because it's warm here."

"Wonderful climate," Jefferson said. "Best in the country. Except for hurricanes, of course. You're not a fisherman, then? Game fish?"

"No. What's this got to do with anything?"

"The doctor was knifed," Jefferson said. "A good many fishermen carry knives. Pretty big knives. Pretty sharp."

"Piersal was killed with a knife like that?"

"We don't know yet," Jefferson said. "Could be. We haven't found it, if it was. You're the fisherman of the family, ma'am?"

"I never," Pam said. "Oh — for the pelicans, you mean? That was just yesterday. A Miss Brownley told me about the pelicans and she was leaving and I — " She paused. "I was just being a substitute," Pam said. "A stand-in."

"Sheriff," Jerry said, "Dr. Piersal was a big man. A strong man. For his age — for almost any age — he was a very quick man. We played tennis with him. And . . . he wasn't stabbed in the back."

"Surprise," Jefferson said. "A knife — a good sharp knife — can be very quick. Somebody you have no reason to suspect. Maybe shows you a knife. Holds it out in front of you. Then . . ."

Deputy Sheriff Jefferson moved his right hand, the fingers clenched as if around the handle of a knife, in a short, violent gesture.

53

He made his point.

"A man could stab himself," Jerry said. "As he fell, the knife could slip out of his hand. Fall into the water."

"Yes," Jefferson said. "We've got a skin diver coming. Only — " He looked at Gerald North. "You'd think a doctor would know an easier way, wouldn't you? Ma'am, did the doctor know you were going out to the pier this morning? You tell him you were?"

"I told him about the pelicans," Pam said. "How they waited, how impatient they got, how each knew when it was his turn — yes, I think I told him I might go out this morning."

"He didn't say anything about going out to watch?"

"No," Pam said. "But — he did seem interested. Of course, he was polite. A polite man. So . . ." She raised her hands, in the gesture of not knowing. She said, "I don't know, sheriff. I hope it wasn't . . ."

She did not finish.

"A dozen reasons why he should have gone out there," Jerry said. Deputy Sheriff Jefferson waited politely. "For the walk," Jerry said. "To look at the ocean. Maybe to fish. It's supposed to be a fishing pier."

"No rod," Jefferson said.

"To see if the pelicans were really there,"

Jerry offered. He wasn't, he realized, going to come up with a dozen reasons. He thought of saying, "To kill himself," and decided against it. Jefferson waited for some further seconds. Then he said, "Let's get it in order."

Always, Pam North thought, people want to get things in order. It is the most futile of human aspirations.

"You got here?" Jefferson said, which seemed to be taking things back a bit.

They had got to Key West, and The Coral Isles, late Thursday — after dinner Thursday. Because the train from New York to Miami was late; because they had to grope, in a rented car, across Seven Mile Bridge, in a thunderstorm; because from the car rental office to the little island which is the city of Key West is some hundred and sixty miles.

They had met Dr. Edmund Piersal, a rangy, pleasant man who was sitting at the tennis court, waiting for somebody to show, Friday morning about eleven. Jerry had played a set with him, and lost it. Later, three young men had shown up and Dr. Piersal had made a fourth with them, a flip of the racket putting him in and leaving Jerry out. The set had dragged on; Pam and Jerry had left before it was finished.

"Any idea who these men were? The doctor seem to know them?"

"I think he had played with them before," Jerry said. "Navy people, I gathered."

"There was a girl dressed for tennis who just watched," Pam said. "A Miss Payne."

"The doctor know her?"

There had been nothing, then, to indicate that he had. But by later in the day he had met her and had arranged with her for mixed doubles, with the Norths if available, the next morning. "Yesterday morning," Pam said, doing her bit to get things in order.

"Yes," Jefferson said. "You played tennis with him and this Miss — what did you say her name was?"

"Rebecca Payne. The poor child."

Jefferson raised blond eyebrows.

"Nothing," Pam said. "She's — terribly unsure of herself. It hasn't anything to do with anything. She — you felt she was expecting to be laughed at. Ridiculed."

"Know the type," Jefferson said. "Then you had a drink with the doctor. Lunch with him?"

"He said he was going downtown for lunch. Some place near the Aquarium."

" 'The Pompano,' " Jefferson said. "Good fish place. Last you saw of him until — last you saw of him alive?"

Jerry said, "Yes." Pam started to repeat the word, but hesitated.

She wasn't sure; said she wasn't sure. They

had danced for a while the night before on the patio; had left early. As they were leaving she had seen a man she thought was Piersal. He was standing, bending down, at a table. There was a girl at the table, there alone.

"I only saw his back," Pam said. "Thought it might be the doctor. Thought the girl might be Miss Payne. Whoever it was, she was shaking her head. I thought the man was asking her to dance, and that she was saying no. But I'm not sure at all."

"Let's go over this morning once more," Jefferson said. "Be sure we've got things in order."

Pam, then Jerry, went over the morning, getting it in order. It was, Pam thought, in the same order it had been before — the same ugly order.

Jefferson thanked them; he said it was all pretty clear. He said he hoped he wouldn't have to bother them again. He said, "Staying long?" and when Jerry said, "About two weeks," he nodded his head. He said the weather was almost always fine this time of year. He went across the lobby and out onto the porch.

Jerry said, "Well," and the Norths stood up. It was Pam who said, "Let's see what they're doing"; she led the way to the porch. They could see the end of the pier; men were clustered there. Deputy Sheriff Jefferson was walking toward the pier. A uniformed man stood at the shore end of the pier, doing nothing, yet cutting off the activity there from the slowly increasing activity of the hotel — from Larry Saunders, dragging his brush across the tennis courts; from the beach boy raking at the seaweed the tide had left on the beach.

A tall, lithe young man stood on the diving board of the pool, bouncing his preparation; in the pool a girl in a white bathing cap looked up at him in evident admiration. The little girl in the yellow dress was dipping her feet in the flat pan of disinfectant solution at pool's edge. All at once, dress and everything, she sat down in it. "Goodness," Pam North said. The young man quit bouncing on the diving board and knifed into the pool. One of the gardeners came, a little wearily, along a path, dragging a hose reel. He coupled the hose to a spigot set into the lawn, and dragged the reel away again, the hose unwinding.

There was nothing to see, except the hotel's life stirring. The Norths went back into the hotel.

IV

The Norths went in to breakfast. They were not especially cheered by Deputy Sheriff Jefferson's question concerning the probable length of their stay. Pam had, she said, got the feeling that he didn't want them hurrying off. Jerry admitted to the same feeling.

"He's got a very suspicious mind," Pam said. "Merely because I find poor Dr. Piersal, and could have made an appointment to meet him there — because of the pelicans, of course — and there was nobody else around, and I suppose anybody could have stabbed him if he wasn't expecting it — where was I?"

"Clearing yourself," Jerry told her, and wrote orange juice and coffee and other things on the breakfast slip. "Just one egg," Pam said. "Not one order."

Jerry knew. Pam is a one-egg person. One order is for two eggs; the ritual is inviolate. Jerry wrote, "One single egg, three minutes," and underlined the word "single." Pam would get two eggs. It would serve no purpose to tell her that she had to eat but one. It was, for reasons rather obscure to Gerald North, the principle of the thing.

The Norths did not hurry breakfast. Absent-mindedly, Pam ate both her eggs. They bought the Sunday Miami *Herald,* divided it for portage, and bore it to the porch. From where they sat, they could see the end of the pier. There was nobody there, but halfway toward shore a bellman — probably the unhappy Jimmy — stood as sentinel, waiting to tell people that the pier, but only temporarily, was unsafe. There was no sign anywhere of Deputy Sheriff Jefferson. The state police seemed to have vanished. But then two men went out onto the pier, and they both carried buckets, and one of them carried a heavy brush.

"All right, Pam," Jerry said, and put a hand on one of hers.

" 'Who would have thought' " — Pam began, a little unsteadily, to quote and he said, "No, Pam. Don't. Quit thinking about it. Read some more *Herald.*" He gave her more *Herald,* of which the supply seemed inexhaustible.

(It was Chicago's day to have an eight-column blizzard. "While Miami Beach basked in eighty-degree temperatures.")

At a little before ten, Jerry suggested tennis. Pam hesitated; Pam didn't know. It seemed, somehow, a little . . .

She was told that that was nonsense. Piersal had been a good guy, a fine guy. But they need not dress in black on his account. Nor, he added, mope. They had come for holiday; for them tennis was part of holiday.

There was life in the lobby now. A good deal of it, Pam thought, was supplied by the sports shirts the men wore. The shirts were not only alive; they leaped up and down and shouted. Pam looked, with approval, at her husband — in walking shorts, to be sure, but above them covered by a dark polo shirt.

They walked through the lobby toward the staircase which would lead them to their room. (In the morning, the elevator was to be avoided; waiters held room service trays in it, over their heads and, precariously, over yours.) They passed Paul Grogan — a partially recovered Grogan. He was talking to a man in a sports jacket, who held a light suitcase in one hand and a black bag in the other. But Grogan saw the Norths; Grogan saw all. He lifted a hand to them and smiled, but only at half-voltage. The Norths went on, up the stairs, to their pleasant room.

They changed. They played a set. As they were finishing, a tall young man and a very pretty girl came and sat by the court, rackets beside them. They sat in adjacent chairs and held hands. As, Pam thought, they had done when they dived together into the pool, when they walked the length of the lobby. Glued, apparently. And very nice, too. Nothing to apologize for; nothing to hide.

"And set," Jerry said, lobbing over Pam's head. Her drop shots today had a stabbing — no, think of some other word. They were effective today. Guile was the answer; the lob was an answer.

"Wonder if you'd care for a spot of . . ." the tall young man said. The Norths did. The young couple came unglued; they were the Greshams. Bob and Nancy Gresham. They came from Chicago.

"Watched you yesterday," Gresham said. "With a tall, elderly man. Doesn't seem to be around today."

"No," Jerry said, "he doesn't seem to be around today. Want to serve them up?"

The tall young man served one up. It was an ace past Pam. "Won't happen again," he said, and crossed over and served again. It was an ace past Jerry. "Never happened before," Bob Gresham said. "Not twice in a row."

But the Norths carried the spry young Greshams to deuce, and it made them feel spryer themselves, and younger themselves; it made them, for the moment and mildly, fond of the young Greshams. They bought the Greshams a drink. "In ball bearings," Gresham said. "In books," Jerry said, and was looked at. "Publishing," Jerry said.

The buffet was set up. It was twice yesterday's buffet, in honor of Sunday. Midway of the long table there was an ice-sculpture — a bird of some sort. Not a pelican. (I'm getting hipped on pelicans, Jerry thought.) Probably a turkey.

They shared a table with the Greshams, learning about ball bearings. And roller bearings too, for that matter. . . .

"Traveling is very educational," Pam said. "But they're nice young things."

They were midway of the lobby, siesta bound, when a bellman called their name. "Mr. North, please. Mr. North."

It was a telephone call. It was Deputy Sheriff Ronald Jefferson. He would like to see them at his office. He would send a car if —

"No," Jerry said, and spoke quickly. He did not and was sure — almost sure, at any rate — Pam did not want to be carried away on the wings of a siren. A false impression of peremptory arrest would be given. He hoped a false impression. They would drive down. After they changed their clothes. . . .

Deputy Jefferson was alone in a large, bare office. There were other desks, empty. There did not seem to be a jail attached.

Jefferson was sorry to have dragged them down. Hated to interrupt people on vacation. Would have gone to the hotel, only —

He did not, at once, go on with that. He said that one or two things had come up. First, he had been in touch with New York. Talked to this friend of theirs.

"I hope," Pam said, "he put in a good word for us."

Jefferson said, "Now listen, Mrs. North" and then, suddenly, smiled at her.

"Very good word," he said. "Seems you've been — well, helpful several times. Very helpful. Said — let me remember — 'When they're around, things seem to turn up. Useful things.' He said . . ." Jefferson paused. Jerry thought it possible the pause was to select. " 'Get them to help, if you can.' He had a message for you, Mrs. North. He said, 'Tell her not to get herself killed.' "

"The idea," Pam North said. "Have I ever?"

"You've come too close," Jerry said. "And Bill Weigand's got a nerve." He looked pointedly at Deputy Sheriff Jefferson, who merely waited for him to continue. "We're not detectives," Jerry said, uttering familiar words with familiar emphasis. "Not any kind. Also, we're on vacation. Also — "

"Of course, dear," Pam said. "The sheriff understands. You said 'one or two things' had come up, Mr. Jefferson?"

" — we'll only be here for — " Jerry said,

and had a feeling that neither Pam nor Deputy Sheriff Jefferson was listening to him, that both were merely waiting for him to finish talking.

Jefferson waited a moment longer, apparently on the chance that Jerry might resume.

"Well," Jefferson said, when Jerry did not, "for one thing — a small thing I guess — it isn't Miss Payne. It's Miz Payne."

The distinction was not instantly apparent. Then it was; Pam phrased it. She said, "Oh. Missis Payne."

"That's it," Jefferson said. "Miz Payne. She and her husband are separated, or something. Hard to find things out on Sunday. By telephone. Going to run Monroe County into charges. People from up North come down here and — " He paused. He shook his head.

The rest, Pam thought, didn't really need saying. Come down here and get themselves killed — that would be part of it. Separate life and death by some fourteen hundred miles; the life which alone can explain the death, when the death is murder. Tie a bronzed young man, who like any other would prefer to spend his Sunday on a beach, to the end of a telephone wire.

"I will say," Jefferson said, "the New York people are cooperating — your friend, Mrs. North. Everybody."

Jerry felt that he was floating by, unnoticed.

"Seems Dr. Piersal worked with the police a good deal," Jefferson said. "It's almost, I got the idea, as though somebody had killed a cop. Know what I mean?"

He looked at Jerry North this time. Jerry felt as if he had been, for the moment, salvaged, or, at any rate, taken in tow. He said, "Yes." He said, "He was deputy medical examiner for a while. Testified as an expert at trials."

"Yes," Jefferson said. "So they feel he was sort of one of their own. Which helps. Miz Payne turns out to be the daughter of some people named Coleman." He looked at notes on his desk. "Mr. and Mrs. Peter Coleman," he said. "Mean anything to either of you?"

They looked at each other. Jerry said, "No."

"Coleman was a patient of Dr. Piersal's," Jefferson said. "Couple of years ago, Coleman died. Mrs. Coleman filed a civil suit, charging malpractice. Came up last fall — "

"I remember," Jerry said. "Didn't remember the names. Jury found for the doctor and the judge — "

"Lambasted Mrs. Coleman," Jefferson said. "That's it. Made an example of her, as they say. Embarrassing to the lady. That was — let's see." He looked at notes to see. "October," he said. "In December, Mrs. Coleman had what they call a nervous breakdown."

66

He looked at Mr. North. He looked at Mrs. North.

"You've met this Mrs. Payne," he said. "What kind of a woman is she? Kind that might — fly off the handle?"

The Norths looked at each other. There was, Pam thought, a bit more to this tall and tanned youngish man — this youthfully handsome, youthfully open-faced young man — than met the eye. He was a young man with a pump. Their minds were, he hoped, wells. If we're going to say no soap, Jerry thought, this is the time to say it.

"She's very shy," Pam said. "Afraid she'll be — hurt. Ridiculed. Laughed at. Antagonistic. I don't think it's more than — "

"Not very well balanced?" Deputy Sheriff Jefferson suggested.

How does one balance a person? A person met, so briefly, during a game? A person who said "Sorry," too often; who said little else?

"You see what I'm getting at," Jefferson said. "You say she's afraid she'll be ridiculed. Her mother was, pretty openly. Then her mother had this breakdown. Apparently, now Mrs. Payne's having some sort of trouble with her husband. If — say she's a little off her rocker — like her mother is maybe — "

"I don't think that at all," Pam said. "Do you, Jerry?"

There was still time to say he was sitting it out. Not as much time as there had been. A little time.

"If you mean," Jerry North said, "do I think she's got a persecution neurosis, I'm not a psychiatrist. But —

"But," Jerry said, "she did seem very tense. Very tied up inside. So tied up inside, so knotted up, that she thinks everything is against her, everybody against her. I don't know what a psychiatrist would call it."

"Yeah," Jefferson said. "She could narrow it down, couldn't she? Figure everything had fallen apart, that the world had it in for her, and blame it all on Piersal? Looneys get funny notions. Do funny things. After all, she maybe thinks Piersal killed her father. It was because of Piersal that this judge chewed her mother out in public. And then her mother cracks up and — "

"If people cracked up from being criticized openly," Pam said, "half of Jerry's authors — "

"Not half," Jerry said. "We get some damned good notices."

Jefferson looked at them and blinked slightly.

"I don't know what made her crack up," Jefferson said. "Maybe she's thinner-skinned than an author, Mrs. North. Anyway, it's what

Mrs. Payne might think, isn't it? True or not. Take her father. He died of something — I don't know what — that Piersal diagnosed correctly and treated properly. That's what's true, apparently. But his wife didn't think so, and maybe his daughter doesn't." He sighed. "What we get down here," he said, "are mostly simple ones. Man kills his girl friend. Or the other way around." He sighed again, nostalgic for simple, familiar things, like lovers who bashed one another.

"And," Jerry said, "she followed Piersal down here and stuck a knife in him? Because she blames him for her father's death and what's happened to her mother?"

"Could be," Jefferson said. "Could be she didn't know he was going to be here and saw him and — had an impulse."

"Haven't you asked her?" Pam said. "You could put it tactfully. 'Mrs. Payne, did you happen to stick a knife into Dr. Piersal this morning?' "

"She's not at the hotel," Jefferson said. "Doesn't mean a damn thing, probably. Maybe she's at the Aquarium looking at the fish. Maybe she's on one of the tour trains, looking at us Conchs. Maybe she's out on the public beach. Maybe she doesn't know that Piersal's been killed, even."

"You're looking for her?"

69

Jefferson sighed again. He said Key West wasn't like New York. He said they didn't have a hundred men to turn loose on it — to turn loose on anything. Or ten men. He said the city police had a description of her and if they ran across her — "when they're not tagging cars" — they'd tell her the sheriff's office would like to see her.

"And the old man's out in that boat of his — " Jefferson began, and his telephone rang. He said, "Sheriff's office. Deputy Sheriff Jefferson." He listened. He said, "That's a note, Tommy." He said, "The hell he is." He said, "I sure as hell would, Tommy," and listened further and said, "Yeah," and hung up.

"City police," he said. "Picked up a con man Miami wants. Man who says his name's Worthington, only it isn't. Miami says he's named Bradley and used to be a lawyer in New York, and got out of stir a year or so ago after serving time on a manslaughter rap."

The Norths' attention was polite.

"And," Jefferson said, and his voice was pleased now, "here's one for the book. It was Dr. Piersal's testimony sent him up. State expert. Bradley said it was one way, and Piersal proved it couldn't have been — anyway, convinced the jury it couldn't have been." He paused again. "Something," he said, and now satisfaction was evident in his tone, "about the angle of the knife. The knife Bradley used that time."

The Norths considered.

"Of course," Pam said, "clichés get to be that way because they earn their keep." They both looked at her. Jerry felt his right hand creeping upward toward his head, where there is hair to run bewildered fingers through. "A stitch in time," Pam said, "probably does save nine. And it's no doubt true about rolling stones."

Deputy Sheriff Ronald Jefferson looked at Pamela North with widened eyes. Jerry could see the young man's hands tighten on the edge of his desk.

"Revenge is sweet," Pam said.

Jerry took fingers from his hair.

"But it may be only prejudice on my part," Pam said.

Jerry put them back.

"It's just," Pam said, "that I've never really been able to believe in it. It seems so — unreasonable."

"Murder is unreasonable," Jerry said, and Pam shook her head.

"Not murder," she said. "It can seem to make sense, I suppose. It's murderers who are unreasonable."

"I tell you, Mrs. North," Ronald Jefferson said, "you've lost me, I guess."

Pam felt she had been clear. She did not, on the whole, see how she could have been much clearer. Which meant, of course, that there was no reason to go on with that.

"Mr. Grogan will be pleased," Pam said. "If it is this Mr. Bradley. Or Worthington or whatever. Murder is bad enough for a hotel, probably. But if it's guest by guest it's probably worse. Mr. Worthington and Mr. Ashley were staying somewhere else."

Jefferson admitted there was that. He said that it had, all around, been a bad day for poor Grogan, what with that Mrs. Upton added on.

"What Mrs. Upton?" Jerry said, and got ready to stand up. It began to look as if they were out of it.

"You hadn't heard?" Jefferson said. "Mrs. Tucker Upton. She was a guest there, too. Found dead this morning. Husband found her. He'd been in Miami. Only, it was just a heart attack in her case."

V

The Norths went the long way round from downtown Key West to The Coral Isles — went up Truman Avenue until it was Roosevelt Boulevard, went around the island's upper tip and down, still on Roosevelt, beside the ocean. The sandy public beach was wide there and people were scattered over it; children ran over it. Now and then, from it, people waded into the Atlantic. It looked, Pam said, very hot, but the Norths are not baskers in the sun. It was, Pam said, too bad about Mrs. Upton, whoever she might be.

Jerry parked the rented car and they walked up the curving drive to the entrance of The Coral Isles. Paul Grogan was just inside, talking to a gray-haired man of medium height, who wore a dark business suit. Grogan's usually animated face was subdued. He nodded sadly to the Norths; even his hair, Pam thought, looked less than usually optimistic. The Norths went to the newsstand and that morning's New York *Times* had arrived. They turned from the stand, Jerry sagging a little under the weight of the *Times,* and Mr. Grogan walked toward them. He said, "Glad to see you got back all right."

It sounded a little as if they had, fortunately but unexpectedly, returned from survived perils. Jerry shifted the *Times* to the other arm. He said, "Back?"

"Understood the deputy sheriff . . . ," Grogan said. "That is, that you — er."

"No," Pam North said, "we haven't been arrested yet, Mr. Grogan."

"I didn't for a moment — " Grogan said.

Pam said, "Of course not. He just wanted to ask a few questions. For the record. They always do, you know."

"Er," Mr. Grogan said. "Does he seem to be getting any place?"

"There's a Mr. Worthington," Pam said. "Only his name's Bradley. One of the men you — chased out yesterday. The men Jerry was about to bet with. On a sure thing at Hialeah. Mr. Jefferson seemed quite hopeful about him. It seems Dr. Piersal once put him in jail. For killing somebody else with a knife."

"I hope he's right," Grogan said. "Although the pier's supposed to be used only by — " He stopped. "Of course," he said, "people can just wander in. I don't deny that."

"Murder," Pam said, "compounded by trespass. But it's better than if it was a guest, isn't it? I mean, for the hotel?"

"I guess so," Grogan said. His spirits did not seem to rise appreciably. "Of course, people get the notion we let just anybody wander around the grounds — "

"Especially," Pam said, "with knives."

Jerry sighed. He put the *Times* under the other arm.

"We were sorry to hear," Pam said, "that somebody else had died. A Mrs. Upton."

Grogan looked at her.

"I'm sorry," Pam said. "The sheriff told us."

"It discourages people," Grogan said. "They come down here to — er — play in the sun. They don't like unpleasant things to happen. They — er — check out."

"We won't mention it to anybody," Pam said. "It was her heart, the deputy sheriff said."

"That's what her husband says, and he's a doctor. He's the one I was talking to when you came in. Broken up about it, of course. Especially since he wasn't here at the time. Keeps feeling that he might have done something — says there wasn't anything anybody could have done but still — Well, you know how people are. Told him Piersal had looked in on her and — " He stopped again, this time as if his own words had startled him.

They startled Pamela North.

"Mr. Grogan," Pam said, "Dr. Piersal went to see somebody yesterday. You asked him to. Was it this Mrs. Upton?"

75

Grogan nodded his head. The acquiescence was, obviously, reluctant.

"Doesn't mean a thing," he said. "Couldn't." He looked at Pam. "Could it?"

Jerry North wished, strongly wished, he hadn't asked. What Pam is asked she tries to answer. Jerry put the *Times* down on a chair.

"Of course it couldn't," Jerry said firmly, and looked firmly at his wife. "According to Piersal, Mrs. Upton had a touch of nervous indigestion. What connection could there be?"

"Well," Pam said, "they're both dead, for one thing."

"Dr. Piersal was stabbed to death," Jerry said. "Mrs. Upton died of a heart attack. Did her husband know her heart was bad?"

"Yes," Grogan said. "They had a ground floor suite. In the wing." He gestured. The Coral Isles had a wing at either end, as if it stretched out arms to embrace the ocean. "Go in right off the garden," Grogan said. "So she wouldn't have to walk up stairs."

"So," Jerry said, more to Pam than to Grogan, "a woman whose health is precarious, who may die at any time, does die. And a doctor who — I won't say treated her. Looked in on her once for a few minutes — is killed. Probably by a man he helped put in jail. What possible connection?"

"I don't know," Pam said.

"People die every day. Every minute of every day."

"I know."

"So?"

"Of course you're right," Pam said. "Mr. Grogan, does the deputy sheriff know Dr. Piersal treated Mrs. Upton? A few hours before she died?"

Grogan said he didn't know; said that he himself hadn't mentioned it.

"Because," Pam North said, "I think he should."

Jerry said, "Pam." He said it sadly, but with resignation. Pam had been asked a question. She would try —

"No doctor," Jerry said, "would diagnose a heart attack as nervous indigestion." He said this firmly. He was not quite quick enough to inhibit two other words. "Would he?"

Pam had been asked another question.

"Jerry," she said, "how would I know?"

We've had it, Jerry thought. And I knew all along we'd had it. Damn those damned pelicans.

"If one did," Pam said, "he might be very upset about it. Particularly if he'd just been charged with malpractice in another case. Even if the jury said the other wasn't. Might even feel he had come to the end of the line."

Jerry did not accept what Pam implied. He

77

said that no doctor who had reached Edmund Piersal's standing, had his record, could also have so thin a skin. No doctor is always successful; no doctor is even always right. A physician, like any other man, may seek perfection, but does not expect to attain it. He does what he can; if he later suspects an alternative treatment might have had more success, he still remembers that he did what he could. He paused, waiting agreement.

"Also," Grogan said, "if I get what you're driving at, Mrs. North, a doctor would know a hundred easier ways. Wouldn't he?"

The habit of asking Pam questions was growing, Jerry thought. It was a most insidious habit.

"All the same," Pam said, "Sheriff Jefferson asked us to help. I think I'll call him up." She looked at Jerry, who looked rather dour. "Probably," Pam said, as much to encourage him as anything, "this man you were going to bet with has already confessed."

"I wasn't," Jerry said, "going to bet with him."

He picked up the *Times,* as a symbol of dissociation. He knew, of course, that it would not work. Where Pam went, there he would go also, to do what he might to keep her out of trouble. And, death to all pelicans.

Only once before had a thing like this

happened to Deputy Sheriff Ronald Jefferson, and that had been years ago. That time he had been lucky; that time there had been an honest-to-God pro around — a state police captain from up North. Jefferson had no illusion that he was, himself, that kind of pro. He was a good law and order man; he knew his town and where, as things were set up in it, the city police — and the Navy shore patrol — left off and he began. But this time of year, the town wasn't really his town. This time of year it tended to be more swarm than city. If tourists wanted to kill each other, Jefferson thought, they ought to do it at home.

It was too bad it apparently couldn't be pinned on Jasper Bradley, alias James Worthington. He was the man for it — had a record, and the right kind of record; had a good, simple motive, whatever this Mrs. North thought of it, and was, moreover, at hand. Or had been.

Jefferson had asked the state police to drop by in Marathon and check, but he had no real hope that they would turn up a flaw in it. Lem Hunter was a reliable man. He had known Lem for years. If Lem said that, at seven-thirty that morning, a man who had registered as James Worthington, and who fitted the description of Worthington-Bradley well enough had been having breakfast in the coffee shop of Hunter's Lodge, having spent the night in Unit 3, the man had been there. If he had been in Marathon at that hour, he had not been, half an hour or so before, at the end of the fishing pier of The Coral Isles, sticking a knife into a man who had offended him by helping to get him sent to jail.

So, in due course, Jasper Bradley (alias Worthington) would be shipped up to Miami to answer, if he could, certain questions the rackets squad of the Miami police wanted to ask him. As a formality, Lem Hunter would, before then, be shown a picture of him.

Which left Jefferson, at the moment, with a looney girl — a girl off her rocker — who might have knifed a man because, indirectly, he might have led to her mother's being publicly ridiculed. Not the girl herself; her mother. Of course, if she thought, also, that Piersal had been responsible for her father's death; that her mother's breakdown, too, might somehow be his responsibility —

Jefferson didn't like any part of it. The county prosecutor wouldn't like any part of it. Also, he wasn't really left with the girl. He didn't have the girl. Unless, of course, she had shown up at the hotel and nobody had thought to mention it to the sheriff's office. He might as well —

He was reaching for the telephone when it

rang. He said, "Sheriff's office. Deputy Sheriff Jefferson." He heard, "This is Pamela North. You asked us to help."

Jefferson didn't remember that he actually had. He had relayed a message from — It didn't matter. He could use any help offered.

"There's probably no connection," Pamela North said. "And probably it's this Mr. Worthington, anyway."

"Doesn't look like being," Jefferson said. "What's no connection, Mrs. North?"

"That Dr. Piersal," Pam said, "treated this Mrs. Upton. The one who died. Anyway, went to see her because the regular house doctor wasn't available. That was yesterday."

Deputy Jefferson thought it over for some seconds. He said, "So?"

"I've no idea, really," Pam said. "Only, if Dr. Piersal, when he heard she was dead, remembered he'd done something contraindicated — like giving her poison by mistake — he might have felt very guilty, mightn't he? Only, of course, she died of heart failure."

"There's that," Jefferson said. "Also, her husband — who's a doctor himself — didn't find her dead until around ten this morning. And Piersal, by then, had been dead three hours or so."

There was a pause.

"It doesn't fit very well, does it?" Pam said.

"Unless he went around early and found her — well, anyway, we didn't know whether you knew. What's the matter with Mr. Worthington?"

"Alibi."

"Probably faked," Pam said. "They almost always are. Did Dr. Piersal have a little book or something?"

Ronald Jefferson felt that he was, somehow, being left increasingly behind. It was a little like listening to a language with which you were only partially familiar, so that for each word translated carefully, five succeeding words vanish like smoke. He said, "Little book?"

"For jotting in," Pam said. "Records of patients. Or even the backs of envelopes. I knew one who did, but he lost the envelopes. But most of them make notes somewhere. So that next time they'll know what they did last time."

Jefferson thought for a few seconds. Then he said, "Oh." There was, understandably, no response to this. "Haven't had a chance to go over his effects," Jefferson said.

He hadn't, he admitted to himself, made the chance. People on vacation do not, in the ordinary course, carry with them revealing records of their lives. They carry credit cards, checkbooks. They can be identified from what is in their pockets, in their handbags. There had been no question of the identity of Dr. Edmund Piersal. It had seemed more sensible to get pertinent information from New York, where Dr. Piersal lived and practiced. Still —

"First I've heard he treated Mrs. Upton," Jefferson said. It sounded defensive in his own ears. "What you're getting at, he may have killed himself because he'd made a mistake in treatment?"

"I said it didn't fit very well," Pam said. "But since Mr. Worthington doesn't fit either.

"It's a bit far-fetched."

"I know," Pam said. "What isn't, Mr. Jefferson? It's a far-fetched world."

To which, after a moment's thought, Jefferson said, "Oh." Pam waited, apparently for amplification. "I see what you mean," Jefferson said.

"I'm glad," Pam said, after another brief intermission. "As you say, there's probably nothing to it. But it's always hard to tell, isn't it? Good-bye."

Chief Deputy Sheriff Ronald Jefferson looked for a few seconds at the telephone receiver in his hand. He put it back where it belonged. He went to the property clerk's office, into which he had checked the more portable belongings of Dr. Edmund Piersal, deceased. He checked them out again, signing

83

a receipt. Items: A billfold, containing two hundred and forty-seven dollars in bills, an American Express credit card, a driver's license of the state of New York, a registration certificate for a 1962 Cadillac, a Navy ID card — Comm. Edmund Piersal, MC, USNR (Ret.) — a scrap of paper with a telephone number written on it in pencil; an envelope containing sixty-seven cents in coins; a checkbook of the Chemical Bank New York Trust Company, with Piersal's name printed on the checks, with a balance of eight thousand, nine hundred and forty-two dollars and sixteen cents shown; a bunch of six keys on a chain; a pair of glasses in a leather case. And — a black notebook.

The notebook was about a third filled with telephone numbers, each prefixed by initials. A return ticket to New York, Seaboard Airline, and a Pullman ticket fell out of the notebook, and Jefferson looked at them, and saw that Dr. Piersal had planned to return to New York a week hence. He put the tickets back in the notebook. He leafed through the book to the last entry, and looked at the last entry. It occurred to him that this detective captain in New York knew what he was talking about when he talked about the Norths. The entry read:

"Mrs. T. Upton. g-i up. hist of 49. Dehy. sl ht. comp. th. adm. dr int. v. adv bl d &

gis. hs MD cf w."

Each letter was well formed, distinct. Dr. Edmund Piersal had written a small, neat hand. If — Jefferson checked back through the book, checked the entries in the check-book. There was no probable doubt that Dr. Piersal had written the last entry in the book; there was no doubt that it referred, as this Mrs. North had thought it might, to Mrs. Upton. Mrs. T — Of course. Tucker Upton, M.D. They came down frequently during the winter, because there was always a breeze on the Keys, and not always in Miami. A surgeon, Upton was, as Deputy Sheriff Jefferson re-membered it. And maybe Dr. Upton, asked, could make sense of what Dr. Piersal had written.

Jefferson read the notations several times. "g-i up." Sounded a little like instructions to a horse. "Dr int. v." didn't sound like any-thing at all. "Hs MD." Husband MD? "Cf w?" Conceivably, "confer with?" It was anybody's guess. The whole thing was.

Jefferson had an impulse — a quite unrea-sonable impulse — to take the book around to the hotel and show it to this Mrs. North. That was evidently absurd. If it meant nothing to him, why would it mean anything to her? And it was she who had found the body. If this New York cop hadn't given her such an emphatically clean bill of health — On the other hand, of course, she had been right in thinking there might be some such notations in the doctor's notebook — the book for "jotting in." Serve her right to be shown what had been there, to be as puzzled by it as he was.

He had reached for the telephone to check on the whereabouts of Mrs. Rebecca Payne, to discover whether she was at the hotel. He had been distracted. He might as well drive around to the hotel and find out for himself. It would be cooler in an open car; cooler at the hotel. It would be cooler almost anywhere than it was where he was. If he happened to run into Mrs. North —

Mrs. Rebecca Payne did not answer the telephone when he called her room. She did not respond when she was paged. With Paul Grogan, a worried Paul Grogan, along, Jefferson went to the single room, on the second floor, on the street side, assigned to Rebecca Payne. The maid had not reached it yet. Grogan said "Tchk-tchk." It was empty; her clothes were in the closet — the enormous closet. (In its earliest years The Coral Isles had catered primarily to fishermen, and had provided more amply for their gear than for their persons.) Her luggage was in the closet. Her toothbrush and a tube of toothpaste were in the medicine cabinet in the bathroom, and cold cream was there, and a box of face powder — Rachel. There was a small bottle of white pills, with a physician's name and a prescription number, the notation "As directed." Jefferson shook a pill into his hand and touched it with his tongue, and the taste was bitter. Phenobarbital, at a guess.

Grogan watched the tall, youngish man. He watched, it seemed to Ronald Jefferson, with some anxiety. Which was, on the whole, understandable; Paul Grogan was not happy about any of this.

"You've no idea where she may have gone?" Jefferson asked.

Grogan had not. There were many places she might be — on the tennis court, sunning in the protected area of the beach, in the solarium. But she had been paged in all these places — except in the women's solarium — by a boy who knew her. The attendant in the solarium reported three women sunning, and one under the vigorous hands of a masseuse, and that none of them, to her certain knowledge, was Mrs. Rebecca Payne.

Jefferson got what description Grogan could give — a slender dark girl, black hair and black eyes, a thin face. "Probably if she went to the trouble — " Grogan said, and shrugged. "She's got a sad expression. Looks sort of . . . oh, licked."

Jefferson called in, found that Sheriff Reppy was still out, fishing. Which left it still up to Jefferson. Pickup to be sent out for one Rebecca Payne, small, dark young woman; age? "Mid-twenties," Grogan guessed. "Weighs not much over a hundred," Grogan guessed. A slight young woman, dark, with a sad expression on a thinnish face. Not much to go on, but what they had.

Autopsy report in on Dr. Edmund Piersal. There was a good deal of it, and it boiled down to one thing: Piersal had been stabbed with a knife with a rather wide blade, possibly a fisherman's knife. The knife had punctured the aorta.

Skin divers had not found a suitable knife in the waters at, or around, the end of the pier. But the water deepened abruptly there; it would take days to search adequately and, even then, there would be no certainty. Piersal might have held the knife himself; falling, released it from a nerveless hand. The knife might have fallen into the deep water. It might equally well have been thrown there, by another hand. And it might, evidently, not be there at all. The murderer might have carried it away.

Jefferson arranged to have the room checked for fingerprints. If they picked up a slender black-haired young woman — and they might pick up several — it would be helpful to be able to prove who she was. Grogan agreed to see that the room would not be entered by a member of the staff.

Jefferson understood that Dr. Piersal had treated Mrs. Tucker Upton the day before. He would like to talk to Dr. Upton. Grogan repeated Dr. Upton's name, rather as if he had never heard it before. He said, "Why on earth?" He said, "What possible reason?"

"Fill in the picture," Jefferson said, as firmly as he could manage. Grogan looked doubtful, but shrugged his shoulders.

He had, naturally, stood by Dr. Tucker Upton, offering what help and solace he could. He had even offered to go with the doctor to help with the arrangements. Dr. Upton had thanked him; had gone alone. That was about an hour before. He expected Dr. Upton to return. He had no idea when.

"Happen to know where this Mr. and Mrs. North might be?" Jefferson said.

Paul Grogan shrugged again. He looked at his watch. They might be in their room, changing. It was about the time people went to their rooms to change.

The telephone in the room of Mr. and Mrs. Gerald North rang unanswered.

"The lounge," Grogan said. "I've noticed they go there."

Grogan kept track of those who went to the Penguin Bar — kept track a little anxiously. He had seldom, in his considerable experience, had a hotel so full of such un-thirsty guests. An almost empty bar is a considerable disappointment to an innkeeper.

VI

The Penguin Bar of The Coral Isles could be reached by going through the dining room or, alternatively, by going around the hotel — past the tennis court, across the patio. Hopefully, the hotel had left, at a corner of the patio, a gap in its fence, so that passersby could enter the bar from Flagler Avenue. Now and then a customer was thus captured.

The lounge — which for some reason was octagonal — was empty when the Norths went into it. The bartender leaned on his bar, looking sadly at the opposite wall, where penguins strutted through a mural. "Birds," Jerry said, with distaste. "This place is hipped on birds."

They sat at a corner table, from which the penguins were not intrusive. The bartender came around his bar to them. "Quiet," Jerry said. "Early yet," the bartender said. It was about five-thirty. At any moment, the bartender implied, hordes would descend. Jerry said, "Extra-dry martinis, lemon peel." Pam said, "Very cold, please." The bartender said, "Sir." He added, "Ma'am." He went away and clattered ice.

"Actually," Pam said, "birds are very nice, I think."

Jerry said, "Pelicans."

"Do you really mind so much?" Pam said.

"I don't see why it so often happens to us."

Pam nodded her head, indicating that she didn't, either.

"We're on vacation," Jerry said. "Thanks." This was to the bartender, in exchange for two stemmed glasses, which had lived in crushed ice before they were filled. "It follows us around."

"Homicide prone," Pam agreed. "It's a very good martini. There's no point in blaming the pelicans. You mean you're really not interested?"

She looked at him, her eyes intent; she studied him.

"Of course I am," Jerry said. "Damn it."

"Of course," Pam said. "Aside from everything else, he was a nice man. Nice to that poor Mrs. Payne. A nice man. And Bill more or less promised Mr. Jefferson we'd help."

"Bill's very free with — " Jerry said, and broke off and looked at Pam, who wore a sleeveless white dress, with a gold band circling either slender wrist. "All right," Jerry said. "I'll never feel the same about pelicans again, but all right. You don't really think he killed himself?"

Pam looked at her drink; raised it and sipped from it. She shook her head slowly.

"Neither do I," Jerry said. "Particularly not that way."

"Because he was a doctor?"

It was Jerry's turn to shake his head. He said that, of course, one would expect a doctor to know an easier way of ending life. But it wasn't that, or only partly that.

"It would be," Jerry said, "a theatrical way to kill yourself. A — showy way. Like — oh, like standing on a ledge."

Pam North said, "Yes."

"If that sort of thing's in you," Jerry said, "it comes out on a tennis court. Dramatizing. Acting it out as much as playing. You know what I mean. Piersal just hit tennis balls. Where the opposition wasn't. To go out to the end of a pier — " He did not finish, except with lifted shoulders.

"Suicide is a private matter," Pam said. "Yes. You don't force it on other people. I still wonder if poor Sheriff Jefferson found — "

She stopped suddenly. "Poor" Deputy Sheriff Jefferson was coming down the staircase from the dining room. She hoped he hadn't heard the "poor." He did not look especially happy, but there might be other reasons for that.

He came across to them. He said, "Mind if I join you a minute?" and sat down. He said, over his shoulder, "A beer, Charlie." He said, to Pam, "You were right about the note-book." He took a small black notebook out of his pocket, and opened it. He handed it, open, to Pam North. She looked at it.

"The light's not very good," Pam said.

"It isn't the light," Jefferson said.

Pam put the little book on the table, where Jerry, too, could see it. Jerry looked at it. He said, "Hmmm."

"It's the way doctors are," Pam said. "If it isn't Latin, it's this sort of thing. To keep things from laymen. What did he tell us, Jerry?"

"Not much," Jerry said. "That Mrs. Upton had a — " He snapped his fingers. "Stomach ache," he said. "For which the medical can be 'gastrointestinal upset.' Or 'g-i up.' And that she'd had them before. Hence, 'hist of.' Since 1949?"

"Or," Pam said, "that could be her age. 'Dehy'?"

Jerry spread his hands. Jefferson reached for the book and turned it around and studied the entry. He said, "Dehydrated?" and turned it back: "I mean, if she had a really bad spell. Throwing up and — well. I'm not a doctor, but — "

"Of course," Pam said. "She was sick at her stomach and dehydrated and — " She paused and shook her head. "S-l-h-t?" she said. "Slight, with the vowels left out?"

"*G* isn't a vowel," Jerry said. "But — "

He picked up the little book and held it to what light there was. "Space between the *l* and the *h*," he said. "Slight something or other? 'Slight hurt?' 'Slight' — hell, 'slight hysteria?' Wait — 'slight hypertension?' "

He gave the little book back to Pam. She said, " 'Comp.' could mean 'compensated,' I suppose. 'Slight hypertension compensated.' " She looked at Jerry; looked at Ronald Jefferson. "Does that mean anything?" she said.

"Not to me," Jerry said, and Jefferson shook his head sadly. But then Jefferson said, "Let me have it a minute," and reached for it. "Dehydrated," he said. " 'Comp. th.' — could be, 'complained of thirst,' couldn't it?"

He handed the book back. His expression was more hopeful.

The Norths were pleased — pleased at progress, pleased with Deputy Sheriff Ronald Jefferson. It was, Jerry thought, as if they had broken into a difficult corner of a crossword puzzle. And as he thought that, his mild elation drained away.

"All right," Jerry said to Pam. "You get all the squares filled in and what have you got? All the squares filled in. An exercise completed, but an exercise without meaning. Mrs.

Upton had an upset stomach, which we already knew. Suppose the doctor called it a 'gastrointestinal upset' when he was talking to himself. So what?" He turned from Pam to Jefferson, and raised his eyebrows.

Hope retreated from the deputy sheriff's face.

"I guess you're right," he said. "We're just working a crossword. Hasn't anything to do with what we're after."

Jerry noticed Jefferson used the first person plural. It was rather, Jerry thought, as if he had pinned a badge on them. Which was — well, which was the recognition of the inevitable.

"We don't know," Pam said. "Double-Crostics are different."

They looked at her.

"You come up with a message," Pam said. "A few lines of poetry, or something."

"That," Jefferson said, "will be just fine."

But he reached out and took the notebook back again.

"Mrs. Upton," he said, "had a gastrointestinal upset, and she'd had them before. She was — "

"Nervous indigestion," Pam said. "That's what he called it."

"All right," Jefferson said. "She'd had it since 1949, or she was 49 years old. She was

96

dehydrated. This made her slightly hysterical, or slightly hypertensed." He blinked at that word. As well he might, Pam thought, and shook her head. She said, "Let me see it," and Deputy Sheriff Jefferson let her see it. Pam made sounds — sluh, hut, or thereabouts. She tried it again. "Sluh. Hit."

"I don't really think we've got it right," Pam said. "It's hard without vowels. Unless you're Polish or something. S-l h-t." This time she pronounced the letters. She shook her head. Then she said, "Wait a minute," in a different tone. "She died of her heart. So — why isn't 'ht' heart? She had a — a what? Slight heart? Sluggish?"

"I don't know," Jerry said. "I still think it's a crossword puzzle." He looked at the bartender, who was still alone, who was looking at him. Jerry looked at his glass, at Pam's. He raised two fingers. The bartender said, "Sir."

"All right," Pam said. "A something heart. For the time being. Then she complained of thirst. Then there was an admiral."

Jerry took the book from her and read again Dr. Piersal's cryptic notes. They read the same way:

"Mrs. T. Upton. g-i up. hist of 49. Dehy. sl ht. comp. th. adm. dr int. v. adv bl d & gis. hs MD cf w."

He saw where Pam had found an admiral.

97

It seemed an odd place —

"Wait a minute," Jerry said. It was his turn. And, in spite of his better judgment — his conviction that Deputy Sheriff Jefferson, with the assistance of Mr. and Mrs. North, was wasting time — he felt somewhat pleased with himself. "Not 'admiral,' " he said. "At least, 'administered' would fit better, wouldn't it? 'Administered d-r,' whatever that is. Administered a dram of — of something called 'i-n-t v.' And 'a-d-v' — of course. 'Advised b-l-d.' "

"Blood, probably," Pam said.

But then, once more, Jerry could see her face whiten under sunburn, and knew she was at the end of the pier again, and that the game had gone out of it. Pam picked up her glass, and finished, in one swallow, what was in it, and that was very unlike Pamela North. It was all right as long as detachment held; as long as it was really like a crossword puzzle. If it turned real, it wasn't all right at all. If it was a man they had played tennis with, lying in his blood —

"Jefferson," Jerry said, "I think you'd better count us — "

But Pam put a hand on his hand and said, "No, Jerry. I'm all right." He looked at her carefully. She looked all right again. She took the little book back.

"You'd think," she said, "he'd have noted down a dram of what, wouldn't you?"

"Int v," Jerry said. He said it again, more slowly.

"Intravenous," Jefferson said, and Pam said, "Yes, I think so. A dram of something intravenously. Of — of something wrong?"

"You're back where you started," Jerry said, and Pam, slowly, said "Perhaps." She continued to look at the notations — at what was the last case history Dr. Edmund Piersal had written, would ever write. It began to look, she thought, as if he had omitted the one detail which was essential, which might now be revealing.

"Advised a blood transfusion?" she said, her tone doubtful. "Do they give them for indigestion? Or, for that matter, whatever a sluh heart is?"

Jefferson said, thoughtfully, "*B* and *l* and then a — " He snapped his fingers suddenly. "Bland diet," he said. "And g-i-s — gastrointestinal series. To find out if she had an ulcer, or something worse. And he planned to confer with Dr. Upton. Why, I wonder?"

"Probably," Pam said, "a matter of professional ethics. They have such a lot of them. You treat another doctor's wife and you have to tell him what you did." She looked thoughtfully at nothing in particular. She turned to

99

Jerry. "I guess you're right," she said. "It doesn't seem to get us anywhere, does it? But it's funny he didn't say dram of what."

"Making notes for himself," Jerry pointed out. "Didn't need to."

Pam supposed so. She supposed the doctor's shorthand might mean more to another doctor, and with that she looked at Deputy Sheriff Jefferson, who nodded.

"Know a man at the naval hospital," Jefferson said. "Ask him about it when I get a chance. But it doesn't seem to lead to anything, does it?" He sighed. "Feel a little out of my depth, somehow," he admitted. "I — "

He broke his confession off. Paul Grogan, his face grave, came down the steps from the dining room, beside a gray-haired man in a dark suit; a man wearing, further, a black necktie. Of all the guests at The Coral Isles, Pam thought, only one man would be so dressed. The poor man. He was of medium height, broad of shoulders; he had a tanned, square face and there was a fixed expression on his face, as if he had gone away from behind it. I feel as if I've seen him before some place, Pam thought.

Grogan nodded at them, without his usual smile. He and the man in sombre clothes sat at the bar, their backs to the Norths and Jefferson.

Jefferson leaned toward them, kept his voice low, said, "Upton. Hate to horn in but I suppose — "

A young man in a red jacket came down the stairs briskly and went to Grogan, who listened, and then turned and stood up. He said, "Sheriff?" and moved to the foot of the wide, short stairway to the dining room. Jefferson said, " 'Scuse me," and went to join Grogan. They went up the steps.

Dr. Upton looked after them, his face unchanged. Then he turned away, looked at the tall glass in front of him, and lifted it to his lips.

"The poor man," Pam said. "The sheriff left the notebook. But of course we can't."

"No," Jerry said, "we can't."

The handsome Greshams came down the steps, came hand in hand. They saw the Norths and smiled brightly, but politely started toward another table. Jerry raised eyebrows, inviting, and the Greshams looked at each other, and came over and pulled up chairs. And after that more people came into the Penguin Bar, and a bar waiter appeared and passed canapés, and gradually the octagonal room filled with sound. When Pam looked again, Dr. Upton had left the bar, taking temptation with him. Of course they couldn't show him the notations Dr. Piersal had made, ask him what he made of them; couldn't intrude. The position of Chief Deputy Sheriff Ronald Jefferson would, in that connection, be quite different. But Pam's hopes that anything would come of it had grown dim.

"Bad thing about Dr. Piersal," Bob Gresham said. "Heard he was shot or something. Out at the end of — "

"Let's not talk about it," Nancy Gresham said.

"Heard some guest went out at the crack of dawn and — "

"Please, darling," Nancy Gresham said. She smiled softly at her husband — her, Pam guessed, very recent husband. "Let's not — "

Gresham said, "Sorry, darling." To either of the Norths who might care to respond he said, "Tennis tomorrow?"

Tennis took ten minutes, and might have taken longer — Jerry launched on one of his doubles theories, which was that the net man, early on, leave his alley open, hoping for a successful passing shot down it by the receiver and resulting false confidence — if Deputy Sheriff Jefferson had not appeared at the head of the dining room stairs. He was tall there, and unsmiling, and when he caught Pam North's eye he jerked his head backward, in a gesture of command. It was, Pam thought, a brusque gesture from a man who had, such a little time before, been almost apologetic.

"Excuse me," Pam said, and Jerry added "Us," and the Greshams moved to let them out. Jerry paid at the bar; Jefferson waited, still unsmiling. When they joined him, he said, "Want you to hear something," and walked away. They followed — followed through the hotel, across the porch and down from it, along the path by the tennis courts and to the sunning area, sheltered by the bathhouse structure. A tanned young man in a white skivvy shirt and white slacks was sitting in a chair tilted against the bathhouse. He was drinking a Coke from a bottle. He brought his chair down and stood up and looked at them.

"All right," Jefferson said. "This the lady you saw?"

The young man — the youth who passed out towels; arranged pads on wooden chaises — looked at Pam North. He looked at her carefully.

"No," he said, "it isn't. I don't think so." He continued to look at Pam. "She was wearing shorts — white shorts — and a beach coat. Blue coat."

"Aside from what she was wearing," Jefferson said. "Could this have been the lady?"

"Look," the beachboy said. "I was way off."

"Whatever this is about," Pam said, "I can always go and put on shorts. What *is* this about?"

"He saw somebody coming off the pier," Jefferson said. "You can't be any surer than that?"

The beachboy continued to look at Pam North. He walked to the side, and looked at her from there. Pam stood very straight, looked straight ahead.

The beachboy went behind her. Pam did not move. Jefferson said, "Well?"

"No," the beachboy said, "it isn't. I remember now. The one I saw had black hair. She was sort of — " He considered. "Lanky," he said. "Little, but lanky."

Pamela North addressed the wall of the beach house. She said, "Thank you. I guess." She turned, rather abruptly, and faced Deputy Sheriff Ronald Jefferson. "And you," Pam said. She spoke distantly. Rather, Jerry thought, as if Jefferson were as inanimate as the bathhouse wall.

"Suppose," Jerry said, "you tell us what this is about, Jefferson. As my wife asked you to."

"Since," Pam said, "you already knew, because I'd told you, that I was out on the pier — I suppose this is about this morning? — and found Dr. Piersal's — "

"Tell them, Roy," Jefferson said.

104

"O.K.," Roy said. "I was coming back with . . ."

He had gone to the hotel store room for his supply of towels. He had done this early, because he had then to rake the beach. "On account of that damn seaweed." He had come around the corner of the bathhouse, with a bundle of towels on his shoulder, and seen someone moving along the pier, toward the shore. A woman — a thin woman, "Lanky, somehow" — wearing white shorts and a blue jacket.

When he first saw her, she had been running. "Trotting, more like it." Then she stopped running, he thought when she had seen him and realized he could see her, and merely walked rapidly.

When she reached the end of the pier, Roy assumed she would turn to her right, toward him, since that was the way to the hotel. But she did not. She went straight ahead, and out of sight behind the bathhouse. "That way," Roy said, and pointed.

"Toward the gate," Jefferson said. "It's supposed to be kept locked, isn't it?"

"Supposed," Roy said. "Only somebody lost the key to the padlock and we had to use a crowbar to get the truck in and — well, nobody's got a new lock yet. Not my job, and I told Mr. Grogan — "

"All right," Jefferson said. "She — this woman you saw — was going toward the gate. And that would have put her?"

"You know where," Roy said. "On Flagler. Right across from the staff dormitory."

"It could have been one of the girls working here. A waitress? Maid?"

"Sure," Roy said. "Not a maid. They're colored. A waitress, sure."

"And you mightn't have known her?"

"They come and go," Roy said. "Here today and gone tomorrow, like they say."

"You haven't seen her since?"

"Not to recognize."

"All right, Roy," Jefferson said. "Tell Mr. and Mrs. North when this was."

It had been at a quarter of seven. When Roy had picked up his bundle of towels in the store room, he had checked his watch with a clock in the corridor. It had been eighteen of seven. Allow three minutes —

"All right," Jefferson said. He turned to the Norths. "Fits the description, doesn't it?" he said.

"I'm afraid so," Pam said, and Jerry nodded his head. "She wore a blue jacket to the tennis court," Pam said. "For the record, I haven't got a blue jacket."

She was, Jerry realized, still slightly annoyed at Deputy Sheriff Jefferson. It had, he thought, been some time since she had been treated as a suspect.

"Or," Pam said, "a black wig, if it comes to that."

Jefferson smiled. He said, "Don't hold a grudge, ma'am." He said, "A quarter of seven could have been about the time the doctor was killed. One way or the other, about the time. She was running when Roy here first saw her. When she saw him, she quit running. But she didn't come toward him, come face to face with him. And — "

"We heard him," Jerry said. He turned to the beachboy. "She wasn't carrying anything?"

"Not that I saw," Roy said. "I suppose there'd be pockets in the coat she was wearing, but I didn't see anything. Look, it's time I close up shop. I'm supposed to start this other job — "

"All right," Jefferson said. "You live in the staff dormitory?"

"Sure."

"Keep your eyes open, will you?"

"Listen," Roy said. "They're nice kids. Some of them are pros. Some of them — hell, we get all kinds. Kids who go to college and have to knock off for a semester to make a buck. I wouldn't want — "

"Sure not," Jefferson said. "But maybe if

this girl you saw was one of the staff, she just — well, saw the doctor lying there and got scared. Didn't want to get mixed up in it. Maybe she's just a kid and — "

"O.K.," Roy said. "I'll keep my eyes open."

They walked back toward the hotel. This time, Jefferson did not stride ahead; this time Pam walked between the two men. Jefferson said, "Don't get the idea that I — " and let it hang there, and was told to forget it. "Had to be sure," Jefferson said, and it was Pamela who said, "Of course you did, Mr. Jefferson. You don't think this girl was one of the waitresses, do you? You said that for Roy's benefit."

"I think one of the waitresses," Jefferson said, "would have told somebody what she'd seen — if she saw somebody killing the doctor, or saw him lying there dead. This business about not wanting to get mixed up in it — " He shrugged wide shoulders.

"Yes," Pam said. "Eyewash. For Roy's eyes. So he'll keep them open. Rebecca Payne, then. Would have gone back to the hotel, but Roy saw her. So — kept on running. Where? In tennis shorts, and a shirt I suppose, and a blue jacket? Without money."

"Like the beachboy said," Jefferson said. "The jacket probably had pockets in it. We don't know what she had in the pockets. As for what she was wearing — one of the few places in the country where it would pass for the uniform of the day."

"Or," Jerry North said, "she could have gone around the hotel and in the front entrance. Up to her room to change. Nobody around at that hour. Wasn't when we — " He did not finish that. Already, he thought, Pam had a faraway look in her eyes. Seeing again, he thought, what she had seen that morning.

"Sure," Jefferson said. "We'll ask her when we find her."

"The poor thing," Pam said, and seemed to speak from a distance. "She thought everybody was against her. Now — everybody is."

There was, Jerry realized — from the tone of Pam's voice, from his knowledge of his wife — an exception to that "everybody." Pamela North had taken sides. She almost always did.

"You'll want this," Jerry said, and gave Jefferson Dr. Piersal's notebook.

VII

It was, Chief Deputy Sheriff Ronald Jefferson thought, all over but the catching. That might take only hours; it might, on the other hand, take weeks. They had fingerprints, now; with New York's cooperation, they would soon have a picture. Eventually, they would find Mrs. Rebecca Payne and ask her why she had killed Dr. Edmund Piersal. Her reasons wouldn't make much sense — revenge for things Piersal hadn't done; murder, you could call it, of the symbol of a hostile, deriding world. Jefferson didn't like it; the county attorney wouldn't like it. And in the end, Rebecca Payne probably would be locked up in one of the places they kept people who were off their rockers.

But if you called it motive, sane or looney, they had a motive. They had her — almost certainly would have her — identified at the scene of the crime, at about the time of the crime's commission. Jefferson considered calling it a day. He could go to the "Sun and Surf" and have a swim, and a drink and something to eat. Then he could go back to his office and see that everything was being done to catch Rebecca Payne — that bus drivers were being asked, and taxi drivers and the car rental agencies; to see that the flights out to Miami had not been forgotten. In short, to fill time, and waste time, asking the obvious.

Jefferson, tempted, knowing he should resist temptation, sighed and felt the small black notebook in his pocket and went in search of Dr. Tucker Upton. Clip off any loose ends that dangled, because the county attorney would, when they had caught up with Rebecca Payne, want them neatly clipped.

("Sure this theory of suicide because he'd done something wrong in treating this woman is absurd," the county attorney would say. "So, why didn't you prove it was while you had a chance? Like before her body was cremated, for instance?")

Jefferson found Dr. Tucker Upton. He was sitting at the far end of the porch, near nobody, smoking a pipe. He did not look at Jefferson when Jefferson came up. Jefferson said, "Dr. Upton?" and the gray-haired man in the dark suit still did not look at him. Jefferson said it again and this time Upton said, "Yes. What do you want?" There was no life in his voice, no interest in his voice. He didn't care at all what Ronald Jefferson wanted.

"Hate to bother you at a time like this," Jefferson said, and Upton said nothing and did not look at Jefferson — looked toward the ocean beyond palm trees which swayed gently in a faint, soft breeze. Varicolored lights shone on the palm trees.

Jefferson told the silent man who he was. He said he was investigating the death of Dr. Piersal.

"I didn't know him," Upton said. "I can't help you, sheriff. I knew his reputation, of course. Knew he was a good doctor. Oh — met him once, for a few minutes, at a medical convention."

He still did not look at Jefferson. Jefferson pulled a chair up. "Yesterday," Jefferson said, "he had a look at your wife, doctor. Mr. Grogan asked him to."

"I know," Upton said. "There wasn't anything he could do. Nothing anybody could do for my wife." He still spoke dully. Then he seemed to rouse himself. He said, "Why do you bring that up? It hasn't anything to do with his death. How could it have?"

Jefferson said he didn't know. He said he did not suppose it had any. He said that "they" — the policeman's invaluable, unidentified "they" — would want everything checked out, even things which obviously had nothing to do with murder.

"They want to have a record of everything a man does before he's killed," Jefferson said. "Who he saw. Who he talked to. Nine tenths of it doesn't mean anything, but that's how they want it. Way I understand it, Mr. Grogan asked Dr. Piersal to have a look at Mrs. Upton because the hotel doctor wasn't available. Sick or something."

"Poor old Townsend," Upton said absently. He did not say why he thought Dr. Townsend "poor" or how old Dr. Townsend might be. "Yes, Grogan told me about it. Considerate of him. Of Piersal too, of course. I still don't see . . ."

Jefferson said, again, that he didn't see either. He said, again, that he hated to bother Dr. Upton at a time like this.

"Dr. Piersal made some notes," he said. "Apparently about your wife, doctor. Don't mean much to me. At the end, something which may mean he planned to talk to you about her. I wonder if you — hate to ask this — would have a look at his notes. Mean something to you, maybe."

Upton drew on his pipe. It gurgled and he knocked it empty against an ash-tray rim. He put it in his pocket.

"I know what the doctor found," he said. "Acute gastrointes — stomach upset. She had them at intervals, poor Florence. Nerves as much as anything. Hyperacidity. She didn't die of that, sheriff. Her heart gave out."

He paused, looked at the lighted palm trees.

"My wife," he said, "was a sick woman. Bad heart. Diabetes. These recurrent digestive attacks on top of everything else. There wasn't anything anybody could do — hadn't been for years. Oh, the things which would keep her alive — insulin. Digitalis tablets on a maintenance basis. She found it restful here, and we came here whenever we could. It was — had been for half a dozen years — a matter of keeping her as comfortable as possible. And . . . waiting."

He did not look at Jefferson; looked toward the ocean, looked at nothing. Jefferson gave him time.

"But if you want me to," Upton said, "I'll look at the doctor's notes."

They went inside where there was light. The big lobby was deserted; guests were at dinner. Upton read the notations in the little book.

"Nothing obscure about it," Upton said. "He looked her over, listened to her. Gastrointestinal upset. Dehydrated and thirsty. Probably advised her against drinking too much water. Especially cold water. Told her to stay on a bland diet and said she ought to have a G.I. series. Had one six months ago. Didn't show anything. Doesn't in cases like hers — functional cases."

"He planned to confer with you," Jefferson said. "Anyway, I guess that's what the last notes meant."

"Probably," Upton said. "Matter of professional courtesy. Tell me what he found. Didn't get a chance, poor chap."

"By the way, doctor," Jefferson said, "did you treat your wife for — for these things that were the matter with her?"

Upton shook his head, patiently. "Doctors don't treat their own people," he said. "Except in emergencies, of course. I gave her insulin shots when I could, because she hated to give them to herself. Most of them do. She had her own doctor — good man. Head of medicine at the West Side in Miami. Anyway, I'm a surgeon, you know."

Jefferson said, "Hmmm." He said, "This 's-l' note. Any idea what it means?"

"She had a slow heart beat," Upton said. "Rate of beat varies with individuals, you know. And, of course, digitalis slows the beat, strengthens it. What it's for. She may have taken a tablet before he saw her."

"And he administered something," Jefferson said. "Intravenously? That what that means?"

"I don't know," Upton said. "Some sort of anticonvulsant, probably. By injection because he thought she wouldn't be able to keep down anything given orally."

He spoke with a certain detachment, as a

physician. He had looked at Jefferson as he talked to him. But now his eyes lost focus, his voice sank.

"She often couldn't when she had these attacks," he said, dully. "Doesn't seem fair, does it — that with all the other things this — this unrelated — " He shook his head slowly. "She never had any luck," he said. "No luck."

He did not go on. Jefferson waited for some seconds, and then said it, because it had to be said.

"Doctor," Jefferson said, "you're quite satisfied that your wife died of a heart attack?"

It seemed for a moment that Dr. Upton, his mind far away, his mind in the past, did not hear him. Then he said, "What?" and Jefferson started to repeat what he had said, but Upton interrupted him. He said, "Of course. What do you mean?"

"All right," Jefferson said. "This is — I don't put any stock in this. But somebody suggested Dr. Piersal might have given your wife something that was bad for her, and realized it afterward and — well, killed himself. In remorse, sort of."

Upton said, "For God's sake," in a tone of amazed disbelief. He said, "Whoever got a cockeyed idea like . . ." He did not finish. He merely looked at Jefferson.

"We've got to check out a lot of theories,"

Jefferson said. "Cockeyed or not. From the look of things, Piersal could have killed himself."

"Sheriff," Upton said, "I didn't know Dr. Piersal personally, as I told you. I do know his reputation. He was one of the best men in his field in the country. Internal medicine was his field. For God's sake, man. He was treating my wife for — my God, for an upset tummy. You mean to say . . . ?"

"Don't mean to say anything," Jefferson said. "I agree it sounded cockeyed. But — I suppose he could have made some sort of a mistake, couldn't he? Injected something that was bad for her, in her condition? Or — just the wrong thing?"

"I think," Dr. Upton said, "that you're slandering a dead man. Of course, he *could* have. I'd say the chance was several millions to one against. But . . ."

He did not go on, but he continued to look at Deputy Sheriff Jefferson. His eyes were a little narrowed.

"There would be things which would be fatal?"

"Dozens," Upton said. "Things that would kill anyone, let alone a sick woman."

"But you've no doubt your wife died of a heart — "

"Wait a minute," Upton said. "That's a silly

question to ask a doctor, sheriff. She was dead when I found her — when I got back here from Miami. I operated there yesterday, stayed overnight at the apartment. About ten o'clock I got back — maybe a little before. She was dead. She might have died any time, and I knew that she, poor dear, knew it too. There was nothing to indicate that it wasn't her heart. Everything to make me think it was."

"Including," Jefferson said, "the fact that you'd been expecting it? I don't like to be insistent. But — look at it this way. If there's an outside chance Dr. Piersal wasn't murdered. That he took his own life — "

"I don't think there's a chance in a million."

"I don't, either," Jefferson said. "But you see the point. Be bad if we made a mistake — got a lot of evidence against somebody when it was really the doctor himself. Bad the other way, too. If this theory got spread about, I mean. Or if some defense attorney came up with it and saw it was spread around. Can't hurt the doctor any more but — well, all the same. You said 'slander.' You can slander a man's memory."

"What you're getting at," Upton said, "you want my permission to have an autopsy performed."

"I guess that's it," Jefferson said. "It's a thing I hate to ask — "

"My dear man," Upton said. "I'm a surgeon. Bodies aren't sacred. My wife lives — "
He touched his forehead with the fingers of his right hand. "Here," he said. "Not in her
. . ." He paused, and there was a break in his voice. "Her poor, worn-out body. I think it's a waste of time. Your pathologist, if he's any good — "

"He's good from all I hear."

"All right. He'll find a badly degenerated heart, probably with the final lesions. May find digitalis in her stomach — she was taking the tablets and sometimes there are traces. They'll find she had diabetes — " He spread his hands, suddenly. "All right," he said. "I don't object, sheriff."

Jefferson had not expected so ready an acceptance. The idea of an autopsy horrified a good many people. It was understandable, of course, that a doctor might not feel horror. Jefferson thought it went further than that — that, at the moment, there were very few things Dr. Tucker Upton cared about at all; that all there was in his mind was a great loneliness.

It was just as well, of course, that Dr. Upton did not raise objection. With nothing really to suggest that Mrs. Upton's death had been from anything but natural causes, Jefferson might well have met difficulty in getting a

119

court order. As it was, the pathologist, old Dr. Meister, would snort, would probably have several things to say about diligent young cops, who didn't care how much work they caused other people.

Jefferson said he appreciated Dr. Upton's attitude, and that he would make arrangements and let him know about them. It did not seem to him that the gray-haired, square-faced man really listened. Jefferson stood up, and remembered something.

"Your wife was dead when you found her," he said. "About ten or a little before. Can you tell me how long she'd been dead, doctor?"

Dr. Upton came back, it seemed to Deputy Sheriff Jefferson, from a long distance. He said, "Not long. Nobody can tell exactly. I'd say not more than fifteen minutes. Half an hour at most. If I'd left Miami half an hour earlier — " He shook his head slowly. "But," he said, "it wouldn't have made any difference. There aren't any miracles, sheriff."

VIII

Pamela North said she did hope that Stilts and Shadow were all right, the poor dears, and that she felt guilty about them. This the first remark of any kind — aside from a passing reference to a need for more butter — Pam had made during dinner. It was, of course, an entirely clear remark.

Stilts and Shadow are the Norths' cats. They were in the New York apartment, adequately fed and cared for, probably bored stiff. What their busy claws would have done to furniture did not bear thinking about, and hence was not thought about. One has cats or untattered furniture; one does not have both.

It was clear. Pam felt, momentarily, guilty about her cats. But Jerry sought a context, feeling sure that one must be there. One almost always was, if one could only find it. It might have been left a hop, skip and jump behind, since Pam's mind skips rather more than some, but it would surely be there. Jerry thought, briefly.

Pam had been silent through dinner. She had done a good deal of looking around. Looking for cats? It seemed hardly possible. Looking at people coming into, walking out of,

121

the big dining room of The Coral Isles; at waitresses carrying trays in and at bus boys carrying trays out again.

"They're a good deal alike, when you think about it," Pam said.

This was not at all clear. Stilts and Shadow are not alike, except in being cats, and Siamese. Stilts walks high and leads; Shadow is a long, low cat, structurally somewhat resembling a dachshund, a comparison which is never made in her presence. Stilts dances confidently through a world which is under her paws; Shadow lives in constant apprehension that something dire will come down on her from above. She is also haunted by the idea that Stilts will go away and leave her.

"Well," Jerry said, "they're both cats, of course. And both seal points. On the other hand — "

"Not the cats, Jerry," Pam said, and was patient. "What ever made you think I meant the cats?"

Jerry considered this briefly. He said, "Well — "

"Shadow and this Rebecca Payne," Pam said. "Always expecting the worst. That every man's hand is against them. Hiding under beds."

It was, Jerry decided, a safe assumption that, as regarded Rebecca Payne, Pam spoke figuratively. Beds were things Shadow consistently hid under, especially after she had managed to filch a lamb chop. That Mrs. Payne —

"It might explain it," Pam said. "Irrational distrust. Of strangers, of course. At least in Shadow's case."

Shadow trusts the Norths, at least when they are not using brooms to get her from under beds.

"The frightened," Pam said, "flee when no man pursueth."

"The word," Jerry said, "is 'wicked,' Pam. Anyway, Deputy Sheriff Jefferson pursueth. At least, I guess he does."

"Funk," Pam said. "That's the word I had in mind. Yellow funk?"

"Blue," Jerry said. "I've no idea why. 'Yellow' obviously is better. Look, Pam. If you merely find somebody murdered, and have nothing to do with the murder — well, do you panic? *You* don't."

"I," Pam said, "am probably more the Stilts type. Among other things."

"On the other hand," Jerry said, making it all as clear as he could, "if you've stabbed a man you had — or thought you had — cause to hate and were seen running from where he'd been killed — "

"She saw the beachboy coming round the

bathhouse when she was halfway down the pier," Pam said. "She'd know he hadn't seen her kill anybody. Couldn't have. Look — "

Pam made what Jerry assumed was a diagram, moving hands through air. She pictured, Jerry assumed, the impossibility of the beachboy's having seen murder from where he walked.

"All right," Jerry said, "she panicked. Which doesn't prove her innocent, does it? On the contrary, if anything. People who panic are dangerous people."

Pam nodded her head, but it was the abstracted gesture of one who politely notes a statement of the obvious.

Jerry waited for further comment.

"Sometimes," Pam said, "Shadow runs and hides when she hasn't really done anything, because she thinks it will look like she has." Pam paused. "As if," she said, editing. "A few days before we left, I gave her a piece of chicken liver — put it in her dish and said, 'Here. This is for you,' — and she grabbed it and ran and hid under the bed, because for some reason she thought it would look as if she had stolen it." She paused again. "She's not a very easy cat to understand."

"A good many things aren't too clear in her mind," Jerry said. "To put it mildly. So? I assume we're still up to our knees in analogy?"

"All right," Pam said. "Over our heads. Although it's there, I think. Anyway — " She looked at Jerry; he nodded his head.

"If people think you might have a reason to kill somebody," Pam said, "and you know they do, and you find somebody has killed the same somebody — you come on his body, say — you might run and hide. Run from the circumstances. Hide — try to hide — from a shadow of guilt in your own mind. Not real guilt. Only the shadow."

"You'd be foolish," Jerry said. "Make things worse. Give substance to this shadow. Apparent substance."

"Oh," Pam said, "foolish is a word — foolish is what doesn't work. This has. Anyway, Mr. Jefferson hasn't found her."

"They'll find her," Jerry said. "Sooner or later. She won't have helped herself."

"You always," Pam said, "want people to be rational. Mostly they aren't."

Jerry said he knew.

"Not really," Pam said. "It always surprises you when they aren't. Instead of when they are. It's ingrained. You wouldn't run from something you hadn't done because it might look as if you had. It wouldn't be rational. So — nobody would. Only, you know perfectly well that a good many would. But when they do, you're surprised."

"All right," Jerry said. "I'm surprised. To get back. Why are you so sure she didn't?"

"I told you," Pam said. "Told the sheriff. Because the motive doesn't make sense."

Jerry smiled. The smile was wide.

"All right," Pam said. "So I've gone in a circle and wrapped myself around a tree. But running is one thing and killing is another. She wasn't the insulted and injured. Her mother was. It's one thing to be fond of your mother — "

She stopped. Jerry waited. After a moment, he realized that Pam had gone away. The waitress came, offered menus for dessert. Pam did not see hers. Jerry said, "Just coffee." The waitress waited. Jerry said, "Pam?"

Pam said, "Key lime pie." She said it from an appreciable distance. The waitress went away.

"There are," Pam said, "just too many steps. That's what it really is. From Dr. Piersal to the judge, from the judge to her mother, from her mother to her. By that time it's . . . diluted."

"To the rational mind," Jerry said, being not quite able to stop himself.

"I gave you the tree," Pam said. "Hours ago. Go on the assumption she's reasonably sane. Just a little . . . quirky. After all, she didn't have this 'nervous breakdown.' It was her mother — *Jerry!*"

"Yes?"

For a moment, Pam merely looked across the table, and Jerry was sure she did not really see him, or anyone.

"With one step out," Pam said, and spoke, for her, slowly, "it's a good deal thicker, isn't it? More . . . solid. The mother — what is her name?"

"Coleman," Jerry said.

"Mrs. Coleman thinks Dr. Piersal was responsible for her husband's death. She tries to prove it and fails and . . . this judge makes a thing of it. Judges shouldn't, it seems to me. But anyhow — the doctor is responsible for husband's death. And for the judge's bawling her out. She goes into a tail spin of some sort. Gets an obsession. Follows him down here and — "

"Wait," Jerry said. "There's nothing to indicate she's down here."

"Or," Pam said, "that she isn't. She could be anywhere, calling herself anything. What's this?"

"This" was what the waitress had put in front of her.

"Key lime pie," Jerry said. "You ordered it."

Pam said, "For heaven's sake!" in a tone of complete astonishment. She said, "Where was I? Oh — I remember. Couldn't she be?"

"Yes," Jerry said. "She could be."

"He — Dr. Piersal, that is — could have told her when he was treating her husband, before any of this, that he often came here in the winters. She could have called his office and they could have said he was on vacation. She could have called here and found out he was registered and — "

"It could be," Jerry said. "We've no reason at all to think — "

"And when the poor thing came down here to kill him," Pam said, "her daughter found out she had — or guessed she might — and came after her to — to stop her. And when she was too late — *Jerry!*"

"I'm here," Gerald North said.

"Perhaps she saw her mother kill him," Pam said. "And caught up with her and — and's hiding her somewhere. When this beachboy saw her, she was running after her mother, not really *away* from anything. What's wrong with that?"

"Nothing," Jerry said. "Nothing really. Only — a complete absence of facts, dear."

Pamela North snapped her fingers, as one who frees them of the irrelevant.

"Probably," Jerry said, "she's in a nice comfortable sanatorium under the best psychiatric observation. In New York."

"Nothing," Pam said, "is more probable

than anything else. Is it a different time here than it is in New York?"

"No."

"Then," Pam said, "come on."

She stood up.

"Come on and what?"

"Ask Bill to find out," Pam said. "He ought to be home now. I'm sorry about the pie."

The last was to the waitress, who said it was quite all right, ma'am.

A northeast gale flattened snow against the wide window in the big living room. From the East River, below, tugboats hooted mournfully at each other and at the night, protesting that this was weather not fit for tugs. Dorian Weigand, who moves with almost a cat's grace, has a cat's nerves when the wind blows. Although, standing at the window, looking out at the snow's swept fog, she did not really move, there was, Bill Weigand thought, uneasy motion in the way she stood.

"It huffs and it puffs," Bill said.

"It screams," she said. "It roars. I hate the wind. I know it is childish to hate the wind. I hate the wind. I'm glad you're home."

It was Sunday; it was also a day off. In the trade Captain William Weigand practices, the two do not necessarily coincide. Nor is either inviolate. To prove this, the telephone rang.

"I'll take it," Dorian said. "I'll tell them you've got the flu. I'll tell them you're blind drunk. I'll tell them service to this number has been temporarily discontinued, due to nonpayment of bill."

She moved across the room, with almost the fluid grace of a cat. She said, "Hello" and spoke starkly.

"I hope," a familiar voice said, "we didn't drag you in from the terrace or anything. It's such a lovely — oh!"

"Pam," Dorian said, "it's blowing a hundred miles an hour. It's snowing a foot a minute. Part of the East River Drive just blew past our window."

"It," Pam North said, "is hard to remember seasons. The first day it seemed so unfair to make the children go to school. Did Bill tell you we're in another one? And is he there?"

"Yes," Dorian Weigand said. "And yes. And if you're calling from Key West to send him out on — "

"Of course not," Pam said. "He told this man to get us to help, but of course not. Can I?"

Dorian held the telephone toward Bill Weigand. He crossed the room to take it. Dorian curled in a chair to listen.

Pam North, speaking from a hot telephone booth in Key West, was sorry to hear about their weather. She knew it was something he wouldn't handle personally. But —

"If it's about Piersal," Bill Weigand said, "we all take it a little personally, Pam. So?"

He listened. He said they might already have it; that they had done a little poking around; that Lieutenant Stein was the one who had directed the poking. If they had poked up anything, Stein might already have sent it along to this "deputy sheriff of yours."

"The one," Pam said, "you sicked on us."

"You *will* find bodies, my dear," Bill said, mildly. "How's it going?"

"In circles," Pam said. "And whether she showed any homicidal tendencies?"

"What we can find out," Bill said. "You're for the girl, I take it?"

"I," Pam said, "am impartial in her favor. Yes."

"And Jerry?"

"At the moment," Pam said. "He's counting minutes, probably. Or fractions thereof. What could 'd-r' mean beside 'dram.' And 'doctor,' of course."

That took a little explanation, during minutes or fractions thereof. "Almost anything," Bill said, unhelpfully. "Just the letter 'd' and the letter 'r'? With no space between? And she had an upset stomach?"

"Yes."

"I don't — " Bill said and Dorian said, "Dramamine. The stuff they use for seasickness."

Bill Weigand passed it along.

"It wouldn't hurt anybody? I mean, to the point of killing?"

Bill supposed that too much of almost anything —

"I'll ask a doctor," Pam said. "I'm sorry about the East River Drive. Will you send us a wire? Jerry's making noises."

"Make ours to him," Bill Weigand said.

Sheriff Reppy had returned, but not to the office. He had had a long hot day; he had lost a sailfish. He was sure that Deputy Sheriff Ronald Jefferson was doing a fine job, and he would see that Deputy Sheriff Jefferson got all the credit for it.

"There's this girl — " Jefferson began.

"Ronny," Reppy said, "I've been up since four. Tomorrow, huh? I've got confidence in you, boy. That's what I've got. Good night."

Dr. Meister snorted, as Jefferson had supposed he would. He said that a qualified doctor, and one who knew the history — and if Upton wouldn't know his own wife's history who would? — would know a fatal heart attack when he saw it.

"He didn't, actually," Jefferson said. "She

was dead when he got there."

"All the same," Meister said, his voice a grumble. "Oh, all right. County pays me to waste time. In pennies but — oh, all right."

Jefferson put the telephone back. He lighted a cigarette. Call it a day, he thought, and not much of one.

The telephone rang.

"About this man who says he's named Worthington," State Police Sergeant Robert E. L. Jones said. "The one we're holding for Miami. The one you wanted we should show a mug shot of to Lem Hunter, on account of if he was in Marathon he couldn't have stabbed Piersal. The one who — "

Sergeant Jones was a background layer. Jefferson said, "Yes, Jonesy. I know who you mean."

"Lem's not sure," Jones said. "Looks like him, only doesn't really look like him. If he had to say one way or the other, he'd say 'no.' Says he could be wrong, but that's what he'd have to say."

Deputy Sheriff Ronald Jefferson said, "Damn!"

IX

The room was hot. There was a small window, high up, barred, and it was open. There was a transom above the door, and it was open, too. Air was supposed to pass between them. Chief Deputy Sheriff Ronald Jefferson could detect none. He sat behind the desk, on an uncomfortable wooden chair, and dripped and waited. They brought the man in.

He was thin and narrow-shouldered. He wore the trousers of a blue suit and a white shirt and no tie. He had a thin face, and he did not look as hot as Jefferson felt. Told to sit down, he sat down, on a straight chair, opposite Jefferson. The guard who had brought him in went out and locked the door after him.

"What," Ronald Jefferson said, "do you want to be called? Worthington? Bradley?"

His voice sounded tired to himself.

"Suit yourself," the man said. "There's no law against using any name you like."

"Unless with intent to defraud," Jefferson said. "Suppose we settle on Bradley."

"If you like," the man said.

"You don't deny it?"

"Sheriff," Jasper Bradley said, and his voice

sounded a little weary, "I've heard of finger-prints. My name is Bradley, or was. After — in view of certain circumstances — I now and then use the name Worthington. With no intent to defraud."

Jefferson said, "Yeah?"

The inflection did not appear to disturb the narrow-shouldered man. All he said was, "Yes," and he said that with no inflection at all.

"You were a lawyer in New York," Jefferson said. "You knifed a man — a former client, wasn't it? Who thought you had sold him out?"

"A man," Bradley said, "came at me with a knife. I defended myself. In a struggle over the knife he was stabbed."

"And died of it. And the jury found you guilty of manslaughter."

"Unfortunately," Bradley said, "both things are true. Also, I am no longer a member of the bar. I'm an ex-convict. Deputy sheriffs can push me around." He sighed, somewhat elaborately. "Sheriff," he said, "there are charges — quite unprovable charges — against me in Miami, which is in Dade County. You're a Monroe County deputy. Are there charges against me here?"

"What are you doing here?"

"Until about noon," Bradley said, "I was

enjoying the balmy air, the refreshing trade winds. Admiring the palms as they sway in the trades. As it says in the folders."

"You," Jefferson said, "are a very smart cooky."

His tone was derisive. But there was no real derision in his mind to back it up. Jasper Bradley did look like being a smart cooky. He also, which was more disappointing, looked like being a confident cooky.

"Thank you, sheriff," Bradley said, and smiled faintly.

"Where were you last night?"

"At a motel in Marathon."

"Why?"

"I was," Bradley said, "considering the purchase of a fishing boat. A charter boat."

"Under the name of Worthington?"

"Yes."

"You have a sidekick. Man named Ashley."

"I have a friend named Ashley."

"You work together."

"Do we?"

"Ashley was in Marathon, registered as Worthington. To give you an alibi."

"Was he? An alibi for what, sheriff?"

Jefferson let him wait for several seconds. He looked at him very directly; he hoped he looked at the thin, confident man with over-matching confidence.

"Murder," Jefferson said. "The murder of a man named Piersal. Dr. Edmund Piersal."

And the man's face did change. The muscles under his eyes twitched; his lips parted a little.

"Dr. Piersal," Jefferson said, "was a police consultant in New York. An expert witness. At your trial — "

"I know who Piersal was," Jasper Bradley said. His voice was quite steady; the muscles under his eyes no longer moved. "I did not know he was dead, sheriff."

Ronald Jefferson felt large and clumsy. He realized he was beginning to feel angry, and that being angry would get him nowhere. He could wipe up the floor with this slight, confident man — this slight, confident crook — who was almost surely lying.

"He was killed about seven o'clock this morning," Jefferson said, keeping anger out of his voice. "When you were having breakfast in Marathon. You say."

"Killed in Marathon?"

"You know damn well — " Jefferson caught himself. "You know where he was killed," Jefferson said. "Here. At The Coral Isles. At the end of the fishing pier."

Bradley merely shook his head. He seemed a little bored.

"You hated him because of what he had done to you," Jefferson said. "Thought that if it hadn't been for him you'd still be a lawyer in New York, not a small-time crook working tourists in a small town — small the way people like you think of towns. Maybe you followed him down here. Maybe you just happened to run into him. Saw a chance to get your own back."

Bradley appeared to consider this. He shook his head.

"Wrong type for it," he said. "I am. Not the emotional type."

"Sure," Jefferson said, and this time did get derision into his tone. "He gets you sent to jail. Raises hell with your life. So — you just shrug it off. Or — maybe you figured he just did what he had to do? Slapped you down because that was his duty?"

Ronald Jefferson got disbelief, ridicule, into every syllable. Jasper Bradley listened as if he found Jefferson reasonably interesting.

"No," Bradley said, when Jefferson had finished; "I thought he was a bastard, sheriff. I had some quite — intemperate thoughts about him. Several years ago. When I was, as they say, up the river." He considered. "In Sing Sing," he said, being instructive for the ill-informed, the yokel. "Sing Sing is up the Hudson from — "

"Damn it to hell," Jefferson said. "Shut your damn mouth."

Bradley did. He used it to smile with. "Wipe it off," Jefferson said. Bradley wiped it off. But the smile was still in his eyes.

He got hold of himself. He was letting Bradley run things, set the pace.

"I'll send you up to Marathon," he said. "Have Lem Hunter take a look at you. Hell — you're so smart about fingerprints. Somebody left prints there. When he registered as you. In the room. This man Ashley, probably. They won't be your prints, will they?"

"Mr. Hunter's motel is quite a busy place," Bradley said. "Many coming and going — just shapes to him, probably."

"And," Jefferson said, "you and this man Ashley — you're the same shape, I suppose?"

"As a matter of fact," Bradley said, "we are, rather. Yes, I think you can say we are, sheriff. It's been . . . commented on. No real resemblance but . . . yes, the same general shape. If Mr. Hunter scrutinized our faces — but I don't suppose he has much time for that, do you?"

"Your fingerprints won't be the same shape, Bradley."

"Never are, are they?" Bradley said, in the tone of one who commends a bright student.

Jefferson looked at the slight man for several seconds, and the man looked back at him, the smile not on his lips, but in his eyes.

"You think you're getting away with something, don't you?" Jefferson said, and anger — and frustration — made his voice harsh. "Do I?"

"This sidekick of yours — this Ashley — it'll be his prints there."

"Will they?" Bradley said, and smiled pleasantly. (I could wipe the floor with him, Ronald Jefferson thought.)

"Sheriff," Bradley said, and there was a certain kindliness in his voice, "I didn't kill Dr. Piersal. I hate to see you waste your time."

Somehow, Ronald Jefferson heard another word, not spoken. "Son." That would be the other word. Or, conceivably, "Sonny."

"Get the hell out of here!" Jefferson said.

The confident, the infuriatingly confident, slight man turned on his chair and looked at the door — the locked door.

Jefferson picked up the telephone on the desk; picked it up with violence. He told the man who answered — told him loudly — to come in and get this so-and-so.

Jasper Bradley shook his head. He made a deprecatory sound with tongue and teeth. . . .

It was hot in the office assigned the Chief Deputy Sheriff, Monroe County. It seemed to Jefferson that it was hotter than it had been half an hour or so earlier, but that was not really true. Jefferson did not get cold with

140

anger. He got hot with it. He was stewing in it now.

Bradley had killed Piersal, all right. He thought he was going to get away with it; thought he'd fixed up an alibi for it. "Probably faked," that Mrs. North had said, and had added that they almost always were. And how right she was! This one of Bradley's — well, by the time I get through with it, Ronald Jefferson told himself, I'll have a hole big enough to drive a truck through.

He answered the telephone before he realized he had heard it ring. He said, "Yeah?" and remembered to add, "County Sheriff's office."

"Jeff? This is Paul Grogan."

Ronald Jefferson got hold of himself. He said, "Yes, Mr. Grogan?"

"Thought you'd want to know," Grogan said. "Mrs. Payne's back. In her room. Called the housekeeper to complain about its not having been done. You remember, you said no one — "

"I remember," Jefferson said.

"A little embarrassing for us," Grogan said. "Didn't like to say it was because the authorities — well, you see our position."

"Yes," Jefferson said. He sighed. "I'll come along and see her," he said. "Soon as I can."

He hung up. The telephone had been waiting for that, and rang back at him.

141

It was a message, left earlier by a Mrs. North. The message was a question: "Had Mr. Jefferson thought at all about Mrs. Coleman?"

For a few seconds that question meant nothing to Ronald Jefferson. He remembered, then. Rebecca Payne's mother. The one who had been bawled out and who had cracked up. And — so? What was he supposed to think about her? This Mrs. North was hard enough to understand when she was there, when you could hear her. Had he thought of Mrs. Coleman? He had other things to think about.

He was tempted to call Grogan back, to have him tell this Mrs. Payne that he'd wait to see her until morning. He reached toward the telephone and changed his mind. In the morning, first thing in the morning, he'd take that smart cooky up to Marathon — take him in handcuffs — and see what Lem Hunter said when he saw a man, not a picture of a man.

He stood up and put his light jacket on. He remembered he'd had nothing to eat, not for hours. He'd drive the long way around, loop Roosevelt Boulevard, and stop at Howard Johnson's for a hamburger and a glass of iced coffee. He'd cool off. Then he'd see what Mrs. Payne had to say for herself. It would be going through the motions. He had the man he wanted — would have him, the slick little shyster. Still . . .

X

Pam said, "Let's have a nightcap," and Jerry looked at her in some surprise. The Norths are not nightcappers. "I," Pam said, "am all keyed up."

"You ought," Jerry said, "to be sleepy. You've been up since the crack — "

He stopped with that, very suddenly. There was no point in reminding Pamela what she had been up since. He said, "Sure. We can both do with one," and they went through the dining room — in which one couple and several waiters lingered; in which a waitress assiduously filled with water the already three-fourths full glasses of the two people who were keeping everybody up. They went down the short flight of stairs into the Penguin lounge, which was a quarter filled. Jerry, somewhat resolutely, did not look at the pictured penguins. They found a table, with their backs to penguins.

Dr. Upton was at the bar, with his back to them — at the bar alone, each line of his body speaking of his aloneness. He wore the dark suit which, almost as much as the attitude of his body, set him apart from the rest — from the men in white jackets and red jackets

143

and, in some cases, lamentably plaid jackets. His fingers curved around a tall glass, but it seemed to Pam North that he had forgotten the glass. Why does he stay here? Pam thought. Surely they have done by now what — what has to be done. Surely there is nothing here for him to wait for.

"Crème de menthe frappé," Pam said, on being asked. "Gin mist," Jerry said and the waiter blinked. "Gin mist," Jerry repeated, more firmly.

Mrs. Rebecca Payne, in a dark linen suit, stood at the head of the steps leading down to the lounge and looked around. Her black hair had been straight the day before; it curled now — impertinently curled, almost gayly curled. That and something — of course, Pam thought. Lipstick — applied with care — had changed the dark girl. "For heaven's sake," Pam said softly, for Jerry's nearer ear. "Mrs. Payne," she said, her voice not too much raised, but raised enough.

Rebecca Payne looked toward them. Pam beckoned. The dark girl hesitated; then she smiled; then she came down the few steps and across the room toward them. Jerry stood up.

"You're sure I won't be . . ." Rebecca Payne said and Jerry, sounding a little hearty to himself, said, "Of course we're sure," and pulled the table from the wall. The dark girl sat beside Pam, and Jerry sat opposite. He wasn't at all sure. He wondered what Pam was up to. Lame dog over stile? Only now the "dog" didn't seem quite so —

"Had to get out of the maid's way," Rebecca Payne said. "I'll have one of those," she said, to the waiter, and pointed toward Pam's glass. "It's aggravating. The whole day to do it in, and my room not touched. Bed not made. No towels. Nothing. And dust all over everything."

"Some sort of slip-up, probably," Pam said. "Something happened to one of the maids and . . ." She let it trail off.

"I suppose that was all," Rebecca Payne said. There was doubt in her voice. "But . . ." She shrugged her shoulders. "I'm sorry about yesterday," she said. "Walking off that way. I was — I suppose really I was mad at myself. When you and Dr. Piersal had been so nice to — to ask me at all. I've been — well, worrying about it. It was so ungracious."

Jerry felt faintly baffled. To have been — he assumed that was what the dark girl meant — worrying about abrupt departure from a tennis court when — well, in view of everything.

"It was nothing," Pam said. "Not worth a second — "

"I know," Rebecca said. "Oh, I do know.

How — what the three of you must have thought of me. And how I — well, how I made too much of it. As if it were important. Or as if you and the doctor did give it a second thought. Only — " She stopped. "I'm tired," she said. "You mustn't let me run on this way."

Her drink came. She drank nervously of a mint frappé meant to be sipped.

"I make too much of things," she said. "Of everything. You don't have to tell me."

Jerry's feeling of bafflement did not diminish. Still, he thought, so much about so little. She had been abrupt at the tennis court. So, she had been abrupt at the tennis court. She was not, except by Pam's invitation to join them, being encouraged to "run on." But to "run on" she was, Jerry thought, clearly determined.

There are, of course, people who must explain themselves, even to those whose interest is minimal. Explain themselves to themselves, with audience. There is a little of that in all of us, Jerry thought. Except, he qualified, in Pam. If you don't get Pam the first time —

". . . ashamed," the girl said, to Pam, who was listening, appeared absorbed. "Just couldn't bear to face you two and the doctor after — after I'd made such a spectacle of myself. It — I thought it would give me time to straighten myself out."

146

"It?" Listen, Jerry told himself, or don't listen.

"It often helps," Pam said. "A long drive. Gets things in perspective. What with all the cars jumping out at you. There must have been lots in Miami." She paused. "Jumping, I mean," she said, partially disproving what Jerry had just decided he knew about her. "Don't you think so, Jerry?"

Jerry put it together. Rebecca Payne had taken a long drive to straighten herself out. A drive to, evidently, Miami. Jerry nodded his head, agreeing.

"It did," Rebecca said, and sipped — this time sipped — her drink. "So much to be objective about, as you say. It worked. Getting up so early, driving when the road was open, the water so many colors. I almost — well, almost forgot myself. Forgot to be . . . ashamed."

She had remembered herself now, all right, Jerry thought. Up to the hilt she's remembered herself; back on the psychoanalyst's couch — the one she carries in her mind — she's put herself.

". . . if you could stand me again tomorrow," she said. "I'd try not to be such a — such a mess. You and the doctor. I hate to ask him, but he's been so patient. About — well, about a lot of things. He doesn't know

I know but . . ."

Jerry listened now; they both, acutely, listened now. What the dark girl was saying was that she did not know Dr. Edmund Piersal was dead; that she had left Key West early and driven to Miami — to straighten herself out — and so knew nothing about anything. And a question arose, popped up: Was it to make that clear she had, unasked, so explained herself?

"Something terrible has happened," Pam said. "Dr. Piersal — Dr. Piersal was killed this morning."

Rebecca Payne looked at her. Rebecca's dark eyes widened. She had lifted her glass and now put it down untouched, so that it clinked on the tabletop. She said, "How terrible. You mean somebody — ?" She looked intently at Pamela North; looked across the table at Jerry.

"Yes," Jerry said. "Somebody killed him. But I wonder — "

"We all wonder," Pam said, quickly. "Everybody does. Such a charming man. Not at all the sort of person — "

That was not what Jerry had been about to wonder. But Jerry accepted guidance. He would ask, later, why it had been offered. And, eventually, someone would ask Mrs. Rebecca Payne why, hearing a man had been killed, she should so instantly have assumed he had been murdered.

And perhaps, he thought, the time she would be asked that was now approaching. A tall and tanned youngish man, a light-haired man with gray eyes, stood at the top of the steps from the dining room and looked around the Penguin lounge. The law had arrived. The law looked rather tired.

Ronald Jefferson, chief deputy sheriff of Monroe County, came down the steps and across the room to them.

"Mrs. Payne," Pam North said, "has been in Miami all day. We just told her about Dr. Piersal. She hadn't heard."

Jefferson looked down at them.

"This is Sheriff Jefferson," Pam said, to Rebecca Payne. "He's finding out who it was. Aren't you, sheriff?"

"Deputy," Jefferson said, and pulled a chair up. "Trying to." He stood, holding the chair, and looked toward the bar. He said, "Hey, Roy," and the bar waiter turned and, across the room, said, "Sir?" Jefferson said, "Bourbon and water, Roy," and pulled the chair out and sat down on it.

Jerry looked at the bar waiter. So this was the beachboy's "other job" — night waiter in the Penguin lounge. People don't look at other people, Jerry thought. Anyway, I don't.

A youth in immaculate skivvy shirt and white trousers, spreading towels carefully on beach chaises; a youth in white shirt and cummerbund of dark red and black dress trousers, carrying trays of drinks. Obviously, not the same youth. Only, it was. Clothes make the identity.

Deputy Sheriff Jefferson, it was clear, was a customer who took precedence. Already, Roy was carrying his drink toward their table. He put it down, and the check with it. "Thanks, Roy," Jefferson said, and then said, "Well?"

"Don't think so," Roy said. "Pretty sure not. Thank you, sir."

"Bad thing about the doctor, Miz Payne," Jefferson said. "Understand you knew him."

Rebecca Payne shook her head.

"Knew him?" Rebecca said. "Just — I played tennis with him yesterday. With him and Mr. and Mrs. North."

"They told me about that," Jefferson said. "Well, here's to you." He drank. "I meant before."

She looked at him. Her dark eyes narrowed, Jerry thought.

"Hate to be a nuisance," Jefferson said. "Rake things up that haven't any bearing. Still — "

The girl looked at him for some seconds.

"So," the girl said. "You know about — "

She stopped abruptly. Her eyes widened. She said, "Surely you don't think — " and stopped again. She turned to Pam North. "He — you know too?"

"Yes," Pam said.

"And," Rebecca Payne said, "you've — all of you have — built it into something?"

There was incredulity in her voice. An intelligent woman, Jerry told himself, can put almost anything she likes into her voice.

"Take it easy, Miz Payne," Jefferson said. "For a while there — well, say I sorta wondered. And you suddenly not being around."

His tone was soothing; there was almost, Jerry thought, apology in his tone. Playing games? Or — Roy had been "pretty sure not." Had that been set up in advance? Pretty sure Rebecca Payne was not the young woman he had seen, hours before, hurrying on the long pier away from what lay at the end of it?

He looked across the table at Pam. Her eyebrows rose just perceptibly, sharing his surprise. She, too, Jerry decided, had thought Deputy Sheriff Jefferson in full cry after this dark-haired young woman. But now that he had caught up with her —

"I should have known it would come out," Rebecca Payne said. "You mean about that — that ridiculous lawsuit mother brought against him? I tried so hard to talk her out of it but — That's what you mean, of course."

"Yes," Jefferson said. "That's what we wondered about a little. For a while."

"And thought — what on earth did you think? That I'd — what? Followed him down here and killed him because — because I thought it was something he did or didn't do that led to dad's death and . . ."

She spread her hands in a gesture of hopelessness — hopelessness in the face of the absurd.

"Well, Miz Payne — "

"No," she said. "Listen. I never met Dr. Piersal until yesterday. No — day before yesterday. I never believed any of the things mother believed. I was away at school when dad died. He wasn't sick long. He died — well, nobody expected him to die. That's what — what upset mother. You'd . . ." She paused, apparently seeking words. "Have to know mother," she said. "They had been closer than most people, she and dad. You could — feel it. Even as a child — " She stopped again.

"You don't care about that," she told Jefferson. "He was dead when I got home. Dr. Piersal had done all he could — all that was over. But not for mother. For a while I thought — well, that she was out of her mind. She almost was. Perhaps she was. She kept saying Dr. Piersal had killed Peter — that was my father's name, Peter. She called the doctor a murderer. She even tried to have him arrested. Nothing anybody could say — the lawyers or anybody — made any difference. There was an autopsy, and the doctors said that dad had had what Dr. Piersal had said he had, and that the treatment had been what it should have been. She just said, 'Of course they stick together.' Our regular lawyers wouldn't do anything, but she found somebody who would and — well, it was all a mess. A dreadful mess."

She had leaned forward as she spoke, had spoken rapidly, her voice tight. She said once more, more slowly, "A dreadful mess," and leaned back against the cushioned wall.

"I didn't know Dr. Piersal would be here," she said, and continued to speak slowly, and no longer looked at Jefferson, or at any of them — looked into the air above Jefferson's head. "I didn't know him when I saw him. I had never seen him during all of it. I kept away from the trial — I couldn't do her any good. I couldn't — If I'd known the judge was going to say all those things I — but there still wouldn't have been anything I could have done, would there?"

"Of course not," Pam North said, softly. But there was nothing to indicate that Rebecca heard her.

"And," she said, "things weren't going very well for me in — in other ways. I suppose I was selfish, wrapped up in myself. I am. Oh, I know I am."

She stopped again, but it was only, Jerry thought, that she had quit speaking aloud the words, the explaining, justifying words, which went on and on in her mind.

"Where is your mother now, Mrs. Payne?" Pam asked, her voice still soft. After a few seconds, Rebecca Payne said, "What did you say?"

But Pam did not repeat what she had said. She merely waited.

"In a place," Rebecca said. "A very pleasant place. She had — she got very upset a few months ago. A depression, the doctor said — a mild depression, and that she'd come out of it. Only, more quickly in this place where — where she wouldn't have to decide things. Where she could be treated. And, I suppose, watched. It's not an institution. Oh, I suppose, in a way it is. But not the kind one thinks of — it's a big place in the country, with lovely grounds — more like a club than anything. It's all voluntary, of course. People go there if they want to, if their doctors tell them they should. And if they have enough money. It's frightfully expensive. They can leave when they want to. I suppose mother will leave before long. When I went to see her last, before I came down here, she seemed fine — perfectly all right again. And that's what the doctors say, too."

She stopped again. It was, somehow, as if she had finally run down. Jerry thought that.

"Watched?" Pam said. "Your mother. You said — "

Rebecca seemed to come back from a distance. She repeated "Watched?" and then said, "Oh. Yes, I think that's part of it. In depressions — well, apparently there's a chance people may try to . . . hurt themselves." She looked at Pamela North. She said, "Only themselves, of course."

"Of course," Pam said.

Ronald Jefferson swallowed bourbon and water.

"About today, Miz Payne," he said, and added, "Just for the record."

"I was a little upset," she said. "About — about nothing, really. I thought a drive would be good for what ailed me. And I'd never really seen Miami — just the airport. The hotel picked me up there. This morning I rented a car and drove up and spent the day there. Drove through the beach area — along Collins Avenue. It's preposterous there, isn't it? Ridiculous."

Nobody quarreled with her. Jefferson did, Pam thought, look slightly surprised.

She had got back about an hour ago. She looked at her watch. "Surely," she said, "she'll have finished by now. It's been a long day."

She made a movement toward getting up. Jerry and Ronald Jefferson pulled the table out.

"It was good of you to let me barge in," she said, to Jerry. "Good of you both to listen."

She went across the lounge and up the steps. Jefferson and Jerry North sat down again. Jerry said, "Well?"

"The beachboy's pretty sure she's not the one he saw," Jefferson said. "Anyway — looks as if you were right about that alibi, Mrs. North."

Pam raised eyebrows, and shoulders.

"Worthington's," Jefferson said. "Bradley's, that is. You said it was probably faked. Looks as if it was."

"And you think he's your man?"

"Looks like it," Jefferson said. "It sure looks like it."

He made the statement, Jerry thought, with rather special pleasure.

Deputy Sheriff Jefferson finished his drink with a sudden swallow. He said he would know more in the morning, and said, "Good night, folks," and went toward the exit. He paused on his way and spoke briefly to Dr. Tucker Upton, who still sat at the bar. Upton nodded his head slowly.

"Had her hair done, didn't she?" Jerry said. "Makes a difference in the way she looks, doesn't it?"

Pam said, "Yes, Jerry," and continued to look toward the bar.

"Didn't mention it," Jerry said.

"No, Jerry."

"Differently dressed, too. As Roy is himself."

"Yes, Jerry. Quite differently."

He wasn't, Jerry decided, getting any place. No place, at least, where Pam was. He said, "Another drink?"

"Good heavens, no," Pam said, coming back. "I want to go to bed."

XI

Of the two, Pam North goes to sleep more quickly. After a time, and usually after only a few minutes, Jerry can hear her soft sleep-breathing, and with that a feeling of security, of reassurance, comes to him. His world is as it should be, turns as it should turn. Then, and almost never before then, he sleeps himself.

He had very little time to wait, that Sunday night. She said, "hmmm," relaxed; he heard her turn in her bed. Then the sleep-breathing began, and with it his own relaxation. The outlines of thought began slowly to soften, consciousness to dissolve. Gerald North, who had had a long day himself, slept.

"Probably," Pamela North said, "it's something in the oath."

She did not speak loudly. It was as if she were continuing a conversation already well set in its course.

Jerry said, "whadga?" and was awake, and said, "What did you say, Pam?"

Pam said, "What?" Then, aggrieved, she said, "You woke me up. I'd just gone to sleep and you woke me up."

"You said something," Jerry said. "Something about an oath."

158

"You dreamed it," Pam said. "Please, dear. I'm so sl — "

"About an oath," Jerry said. "You spoke quite clearly."

"All right," Pam said. "I was talking in a dream. Please, Jerry. I'm so . . ."

And again her breathing was the slow, just audible, breathing of one who sleeps.

Jerry puzzled for a few minutes. It is not usual for Pam to "talk in a dream." But it is not unheard of. She had had a long, disturbing day. The disturbance had lasted into sleep. That was all it was. Jerry could not remember that, during the day, there had been any special amount of swearing, but — It'll all come out in the wash, Jerry thought, and knew, vaguely, that he did not mean wash, but meant morning, and sleep recaptured him.

"I never see why the glass doesn't break," Pamela North said, at a little after eight o'clock Monday morning. She was wearing a short nightgown and was pleasantly visible through it. She was watching a glass of water into which the gadget had been inserted. The gadget was doing its electrical duty; the water in the glass bubbled. Pam took the gadget out quickly and put it in the other glass. She was supposed to detach it between glasses; it had said so on the directions. This was something Jerry had given up mentioning. She put powdered coffee and a cream substitute in the first glass and wrapped it in facial tissue and carried it to Jerry, who propped himself up and took the glass and said, "Ouch. Thank you."

"But they never do," Pam said, and disconnected the gadget and took it out of the other glass, and made instant coffee again and picked it up in tissue — and said, "Ouch" — and carried it to her own bed.

"You can *still* taste the chlorine," Pam said, after tasting. "Right through everything."

"It's fine coffee," Jerry said. "You were talking in your sleep last night."

"I'm sorry. About what?" She sipped again. "Because," she said, "I hope I didn't miss anything interesting."

"Obscure," Jerry said. "Something about something's being in an oath."

"I couldn't have."

Jerry lighted a cigarette. "It's before breakfast," Pam said. Jerry pointed at his glass. "That's cheating," Pam said. "Also, there's a Florida law against smoking in bed. It says so on the card."

"Enforceable," Jerry said, "after you've burned up. Unless they make surprise bed checks from time to time."

"An embarrassing thought," Pam said. "Aren't you going to light me one?"

He lighted her one. He said, "You don't

remember anything about it?"

"No. I was dreaming something. I don't know what. If I really — "

"Yes. You said, 'Probably it's something in the oath.' "

"I've no idea," Pam said. "I never remember dreams, you know. You ought to be glad. I've been reading *The Will of Zeus*. Lovely book, but people in it are always making oaths of one sort and another. To soften up the gods, mostly. Probably it was that. More instant chlorine?"

She made more coffee. Jerry watched her with pleasure. They drank more coffee. They debated whether to have breakfast sent up, and on other matters of importance — should they, if they decided to go down for breakfast, dress for tennis or for going down to breakfast? Was this the day they would drive up to Marathon and lunch at Hanley's, where people said there were always stone crabs? Holidays are times for decisions.

The decisions were for going down — "because it takes forever, and everything's cold" — and against dressing for tennis. "Because we can't tell what may come up."

They walked along the corridor toward the stairs, and a rotund man in a very noticeable sports shirt came toward them. He carried a physician's black bag; he had a border of white hair around a sunburned head; he walked, Pam thought, with the resolute youth of a man who knows himself aging. Before he reached them he stopped at a door and knocked and then, in answer to something they did not hear, "Dr. Townsend, Mr. Porter." He had a hearty voice. As they passed him, still waiting for the door to open, he gave them a brief and hearty nod, and a smile to go with it.

"Doctor's back on his feet again, apparently," Jerry said, when they were going down the stairs.

"I hope we don't get sick," Pam said, and they walked the long length of the lobby toward the dining room. They picked up the Miami *Herald*. Dr. Tucker Upton, his tanned face without expression, came out of a telephone booth and walked toward Paul Grogan at the desk.

"There's something on the tip of my mind," Pam said. "Only it keeps falling off."

· "About an oath?"

She didn't think so. Nothing about an oath seemed to come into it. She still thought she must have been dreaming about Greeks. She also thought she would have wheat cakes and sausage.

"And," Jerry said, "the hell with it."

"Precisely."

They were drinking coffee and smoking —

this time legally, breakfast being past — when a boy brought them a telegram. It read:

"Mrs. Peter Coleman left Green Acres, private sanitarium, own volition ten days ago. Voluntary patient. Mild depression, marked improvement doctor says. Is in fifties, black hair and eyes, wt. 120. About five-four. Good fig. Returned apartment but left week ago. Mail to be forwarded her attorney. Maid denies knowledge employer's whereabouts but thinks quote somewhere South unquote. Says plays races. Re daughter. Husband is in Washington, says she South for rest, denies separation. Don't stick necks out too far. Wish we were there. Bill."

"As if we ever do," Pam said. "She could be here, then."

"Or a hundred places. There's no racing here."

"Dogs," Pam said. "But you're probably right. Still . . ."

Still — Jerry called the office of the Monroe County sheriff to report that one Mrs. Peter Coleman was, in a manner of speaking, on the loose. Chief Deputy Sheriff Ronald Jefferson had been in and gone out. Sheriff Reppy, on the other hand, had not yet come in. A message was taken.

The Norths went to the porch to read the Miami *Herald*. Winter was "on a rampage"

163

in the Middle West.

Ronald Jefferson had awakened and found himself on top of the world. He was usually there, or thereabouts, on awakening, but this morning he felt especially exuberant. After a few minutes — and a cup of coffee — he realized why. He was going to take that supercilious little bastard up to Marathon and watch him squirm. It was going to be a fine day, and probably the last day of this particular mess.

He was glad, on the whole, that the dark girl was out of it. He didn't like cracking down on ladies if it could be avoided. There was, to be sure, the girl Roy had seen — the girl in white shorts and a blue jacket. But she probably hadn't had anything to do with it. She'd been for a dip in the salt-water pool. Maybe she'd slipped in from outside, trespassed on hotel property. That would account for her getting out fast when she was seen.

It was, Jefferson told himself as he drove to his office, narrowing down nicely.

Sheriff Reppy hadn't got in yet. That was all right, too. The old boy wasn't always in good humor after a day of fishing, particularly when the big one had got away. The old boy might want, in spite of what he had said, to put an oar in. Not that he often did, but still —

There were other deputies around now, with Sunday over. Now that there was nothing much to do, there were plenty to do it. Jefferson sent one of them to get a car and take it to the jail entrance, told him they were going to take a little ride up to Marathon.

He had wasted a good deal of time yesterday, Jefferson thought. With those Norths, who hadn't really helped much — she had suggested the alibi was faked, but he'd have come on that without her. With Dr. Upton, the poor guy. It was obvious, now, that Upton didn't come into it at all, that Dr. Piersal's professional visit to Mrs. Upton had nothing to do with anything. It was the Norths, come to think of it, who had led him up that blind alley. Nice people, but given, as amateurs were, to going up blind alleys. Which reminded Deputy Sheriff Jefferson.

He called the morgue. No use in going on with that autopsy on poor Mrs. Upton. The old boy wouldn't have started yet.

The old boy, which was to say Dr. Ferdinand Meister, had started. He sent out word: "Tell him I'm working on his cadaver." The wording gave Deputy Jefferson a momentary start.

It was, Jefferson decided, hanging up the telephone, probably just as well. Nothing would come of it, but if a defense attorney

165

got to nosing around, the way defense attorneys did, it would do no harm to be able to say, "Oh, but we did think of that, counsellor. Left no stone unturned, counsellor. Results negative, of course."

He checked with the state police. Matters were in hand.

The narrow-shouldered man was ready at the jail. He wore a blue suit and a white shirt and a necktie — a conservative necktie. He looked quite cool and quite confident. But this time Jefferson had no intention of letting that get his goat. (He'd been tired, yesterday; hot and tired.)

"Going to take you for a little ride up to Marathon," he told Jasper Bradley, small-time crook who'd stepped over the line into the biggest time there was.

"It's a pretty drive," Bradley said. "Don't tell me you're going along yourself, sheriff."

There was nothing really out of the way about what Bradley said, nor in the way he said it. No ridicule. Nothing to get a man's goat, not really. And when Jefferson cuffed Bradley to him, Bradley's right wrist to his left, there was again nothing out of the way in Bradley's attitude. He sighed, as a man so fettered might well. There was really nothing to suggest that it was a man's tolerant sigh over another's boyish behavior.

166

"Let's get going," Jefferson said, his voice rough. (The man rubbed him the wrong way; he was letting himself be rubbed the wrong way.) "If you're ready, mister," he added.

They sat in the back seat while Deputy Williams drove. On Stock Island Williams used his siren once or twice.

"No hurry, Willie," Jefferson told him. "Mr. Bradley says it's a pretty ride. Give him time to enjoy it."

That was the way to play it.

It is fifty miles or so from Key West to Marathon, and it is a very pretty ride indeed — a ride with water on either side, water which is iridescent in the mornings, water which changes color before the eyes; which is green and blue and a dozen shadings of green and blue; water over which white birds circle, on the shores of which white birds stand on legs breathtakingly fragile. Pelicans chug above the varicolored waters and gulls coast and dive. Far to the right as one drives north and east the water is the deepest blue of all, and that is the Gulf Stream, just beginning its journey to far places.

Jasper Bradley, disbarred lawyer and small-time crook, on his way to have an alibi broken so he could be tried for Murder One, seemed to enjoy the beauty of sea and sky very much indeed. It was a morning of puffy clouds, and

Bradley commented on the serene charm of such formations. He was also audibly delighted by the water's shifting hues.

He was, in all respects, a most appreciative guest. Ronald Jefferson could have throttled him.

There are numerous motels in Marathon, from the simplest, which announce their overnight rates on their signs and are even, in some cases, permissive of house trailers, to those which mention pools and cocktail lounges and golf privileges, and consider public mention of rates vulgar. The names of some are fanciful, and often have to do with pirates. (Self-criticism is not intended; the reference is to ancient days, when buccaneers did foray from the Keys.)

Lem Hunter's motel was comparatively austere. It announced itself as "Hunter's Lodge," and its sign's only other comment was, "Entrance." It was on the Gulf side, just visible from the road. Its beach was on the Gulf; palms shaded its fresh-water pool.

Deputy Williams stopped the official car in front of the door marked "Office." Chief Deputy Jefferson said, "End of the line, Bradley," and slid toward the door. Bradley, perforce, slid with him.

Bradley said, "Of course, it's up to you, sheriff. I quite realize that. Only — these."

He lifted his right arm, shook it slightly so the chain between them clicked.

"What about them?" Jefferson said. "You don't like them, mister?"

"Not especially," Bradley said. "But I wasn't thinking of that. However, the point has probably occurred to you already."

Jefferson tried to stop himself. He was not in time. He said, "What're you getting at?"

"You want an identification," Bradley said. "Preferably, of course, you want no identification. You hope that Mr. Hunter will say he has never seen me before. Eventually, you no doubt hope to bring his identification, or non-identification, into court."

"So?"

His voice was very harsh on "So." He somehow got a "z" sound into it.

"I didn't mean to annoy you," Bradley said. "It was quite presumptuous of me, under the circumstances. I realize that, sheriff. And that you know your business. I don't question that."

He was at it again, Jefferson realized. He was — damn it to hell, Jefferson thought. It's like he was patting me on the head, because I'm such a good little boy.

"What the hell you getting at?" Jefferson said. He had tried not to.

"Nothing, really," Bradley said. "I'm sure

169

you've often given evidence in court, sheriff. Know how niggling little points get dragged in. What a lot lawyers try to make out of nothing." He sighed, apparently at the habits of attorneys. "I was quite bad at that — or good, looking at it another way — in the old days. I'm afraid I would have made quite a point of the handcuffs, sheriff. Unfairly, perhaps. But that's the way things are, isn't it?"

"What point?" Jefferson said. He kept his voice harsh, but he asked.

"Oh," Bradley said. "I'm sure you've thought of it, sheriff. As an experienced law officer. Prejudice would be a word for it. Prejudicial circumstances. Mr. Hunter picked this man out — or didn't pick him out — from among several other men? A lawyer will almost certainly ask something like that. No. That would have to be your answer, wouldn't it? The lawyer would look surprised, you know. Shocked, even. He'd look at the jury long enough to let them see how shocked he was. Then he'd say — I'm remembering how I used to do these things, sheriff — 'Suppose you tell us the circumstances of this identification, sheriff?' So you say, 'Well, I dragged him up to the desk and — ' and the lawyer says, 'Dragged? Just what do you mean, dragged, sheriff?' And you say, 'Well, I had handcuffs on him and — ' " Bradley broke off to sigh; the sigh was clearly one of pity.

"He makes quite a point of it, I'm afraid," Bradley said. "This lawyer. You know how lawyers are. 'Did you expect this Mr. Hunter to take an impartial look at a man you had in handcuffs, sheriff? Did you expect a dispassionate decision? You didn't know — didn't dream — that because this man was chained to you, Mr. Hunter — anyone — would be prejudiced against him? Would say to himself, "Sure, this is the guilty man. Probably dangerous, too. Otherwise, why does this sheriff — who'd make two of him — put the cuffs on him?" ' Then the lawyer moves to have the evidence of identification — or non-identification — ruled inadmissible and the judge — "

He paused. He shrugged. "Of course," Jasper Bradley said, "I've never been a judge." He smiled at Jefferson. "But obviously," he said, "you've thought of all this. I realize that — "

Jefferson hadn't thought of all that. That was what this skinny little — That was what Jasper Bradley, small-time con man, realized. That was what he was needling Deputy Sheriff Jefferson about.

And probably there was something to it. Why the little bastard should point it out, except that he couldn't keep his mouth shut,

171

couldn't put the needle away — All the same, there might be something to it. Jefferson thought of Judge Ackerman. When it came to trial, the charge murder in the first degree, it would almost certainly come up before Judge Ackerman. And the way Ackerman acted sometimes you'd think he didn't like cops, enjoyed putting cops in the wrong. "Prejudicial to the rights of the defendant." That was the sort of thing Judge Ackerman liked to say, even when nobody had laid hands on somebody everybody knew was guilty as hell. Just maybe kept him awake when he wanted to go to sleep, or some ordinary thing like that.

"Trying to get away with something, aren't you?" Jefferson said, in his roughest voice. But it didn't really, in his own ears, sound very good or even, come to that, very rough.

Bradley sighed again. This was the sigh of a man misunderstood; of a man who has sought merely to help, and has been rebuffed.

So, Jefferson thought, probably there was something in what the little so-and-so said. And there was something else. Suppose Bradley wanted the cuffs off so he could make a break for it. If a man trying to escape gets roughed up a little, nobody can make a point of that. Not shot, not really hurt. Ronald Jefferson had never, in fact, shot anyone, al-

172

though he had shot over a few heads. He had never actually roughed anybody up, either — not unless somebody else started the roughing, and then only enough to stop that. Well, there could always be a first time. Let this smart-aleck give him an excuse —

Jasper Bradley looked as if he wanted to smile, and was restraining himself, out of consideration. Smile or, come to that, laugh.

"Don't try anything," Jefferson said. "Just don't try anything."

He unlocked the handcuffs and put them in his pocket. Bradley rubbed his wrist. He looked up and down Ronald Jefferson, looked at his own thin hands. Again he sighed, a man resigned to the unreasonableness of others.

Williams stayed in the car. Jefferson took the thin man into the office, a big hand hard on a thin arm. Lemuel Hunter was behind the desk. He was a thin man, too — a hard thin man, with white hair and a face deeply tanned. He wore a blue polo shirt and dark slacks. He said, "Good morning, Jeff," and New England was in the timbre of his voice, in his inflection. (When Ronald Jefferson had first met Lem Hunter some years earlier he had decided that Hunter was some kind of foreigner.)

Hunter looked at Jefferson and then, longer, at Jasper Bradley. There was nothing

173

to show that this bothered Bradley. Hunter said, " 'Morning," and Bradley said, "Good morning, Mr. Hunter."

"Man you sent me the picture of, isn't he?" Hunter said, and Jefferson said, "Yeah," and Bradley said nothing at all.

"Saturday evening," Hunter said, "they came in pretty fast. Check-outs Saturday morning; check-ins Saturday night. Abby gives me a hand."

"I know, Lem," Jefferson said.

"Name of Worthington?"

"That's the name he — " Jefferson caught himself. He was looking at Hunter, not at the skinny little — But he could feel that Jasper Bradley was, again, on the verge of smiling. The smile would be one of pity. Conduct prejudicial to the rights —

"Yes," Jefferson said, "that's the name."

He did not look at Bradley.

"Wonder," Hunter said, "if you'd mind going over to the door and walking back, Mr. Worthington?"

If he's looking for a chance, this'll give it to him, Ronald Jefferson thought. But Williams is outside. He won't forget Williams.

"Certainly," Bradley said, and walked to the door. He turned and walked back again. He limped slightly. "Cramp in my leg," he said. "Get it when I sit in one position for long.

Sometimes I do."

"Yep," Hunter said. "About six-thirty, maybe. Next to the last room. Number 11, that was. Overnight. Don't get many overnighters, you know. Don't cater to them, especially. But — yes, Jeff. Checked him in myself."

Jefferson continued not to look at Jasper Bradley, not to see whether he was smiling. If he was smiling, the little —

"You weren't so sure when you saw the photograph," Jefferson said.

"No," Hunter said. "Picture's one thing. Seein's another."

"You'd swear to it?"

"Yep," Hunter said. " 'Fraid I would, Jeff."

"Because of the limp?"

"Could be. Could be that helps. But mostly that just brings the situation back. See what I mean? The picture."

"Yeah," Jefferson said. "I guess I do, Lem."

"You thought he wouldn't be? That somebody else used his name?"

"Far as the name goes — " Jefferson said, and caught himself again, and said, "Yeah. That's it."

" 'Fraid not," Hunter said. "This man's Mr. Worthington, who checked in Saturday evening. By the way, state cops left this for you, Jeff."

He took an envelope out of a pigeonhole in the letter rack. Jefferson opened it, but he knew, feeling no enthusiasm, what it would be.

It was not a full report from the state police fingerprint boys. That would go on, through channels, to the office. It was enough. Prints on the registration card those of Jasper Bradley, alias James Worthington. (Together with those of Lemuel Hunter, owner-manager of Hunter's Lodge.) Prints in Room 11, assigned Bradley, those of Bradley. (And of other people, presumably previous occupants, in several instances underlying those of Bradley.) Jefferson put the report back in its envelope, and the envelope in his pocket. He was aware that Bradley was looking at him, and did not look at Bradley. Jefferson said, "Well — " and heard reluctance in his voice, and thought of something.

"Pay in advance for the night?" Jefferson asked Lem Hunter, and Hunter shook his head.

"Don't operate that way here," he said, and there seemed to be faint distaste in his voice. "Not exactly a roadside stopover."

"Then in the morning he'd have to check out, pay his bill."

"Did that," Hunter said. "Had breakfast, charged it on his bill, paid his bill. Checked out about — about when was it, Mr. Worthington?"

"Eight-thirty," Bradley said, pleasantly. "Between that and nine."

Jefferson turned to Bradley, then — turned abruptly.

"Mind saying what you had for breakfast?" Jefferson said.

And Bradley smiled. (That damned, tolerant smile!) He said, "Not at all, sheriff. Scrambled eggs, bacon, toast and coffee. Oh, and orange juice. All very good, too."

The check would show what had been eaten by the occupant of Room 11 at breakfast Sunday morning. If it had not been destroyed. And it would show scrambled eggs and bacon and toast and coffee. And orange juice.

"Held onto it after I got your query," Hunter said, and reached into another pigeonhole and came out with several papers and shuffled them, and put one down on the desk in front of Jefferson. It was a charge slip for breakfast, eaten the previous morning. The items were those Jefferson had known they would be. He looked at Bradley. Bradley's expression was one of sympathy. Jefferson felt somewhat like a large puppet, dangled on strings held in expert fingers. The skinny, crooked, little —

"You check him out, Lem?"

Hunter hadn't. A man had to get some sleep sometime. Abby — that would be Mrs. Abigail Hunter — had been on the desk then. She'd be out checking with the restaurant manager now, but if Jeff wanted —

Jefferson said, "If it isn't too much trouble. Hate to bother Miz Hunter but — "

They waited a few minutes after Hunter used the telephone. Mrs. Hunter came in. She was a largish woman, noticeably well-corseted. Jefferson said, " 'Morning, Miz Hunter. Ever see this man before?"

She looked at Bradley. She shrugged her shoulders. She said, "See a lot, sheriff. Come and go. When?"

"Yesterday morning, Abby," Hunter said. "Checkout. Eleven. Twenty-three sixty-nine, counting tax."

She looked at Bradley again, shrugged again. She said, "People getting mail, people asking how to get places, people wanting the wagon for the golf course."

"I know," Lem Hunter said.

"Gave me a twenty and a five," Mrs. Hunter said. "Looked at the twenty because there's a list out. Wasn't on the list. Wasn't counterfeit far's I could see." She looked at her husband, with some anxiety.

"No," Hunter said. "The bill was all right."

"About the man, Miz Hunter?"

She looked at Bradley again, and once more shrugged her shoulders.

"Looks sort of familiar," she said. "Thin man, seems I remember. Like he is."

"Remember whether the man who checked out limped, Miz Hunter?"

"Can't say I do," Mrs. Hunter said. "One way or the other." She waited a few moments. She said, "That all, sheriff? Because I've got things to do."

"I guess it is," Jefferson said, and Abigail Hunter went, briskly, to do the things she had to do.

Jasper Bradley, alias Worthington, was again appreciative, as they drove back to Key West, of the beauty around them. Driving with the sun at their backs, the colors were quite different, but no less exciting to the eye. Had Sheriff Jefferson noted the difference?

"Shut your yap, for God's sake," Sheriff Jefferson told him. "And wipe that smile off."

Bradley said, "Certainly, sheriff," and did.

When he got out of the car, and was taken into the jail by Deputy Williams, while Jefferson sat and watched, and thought what he'd like to do to the little so-and-so, Bradley limped. He hadn't when they walked from motel office to the car.

The "cramp" had obviously — a hell of a lot too obviously — recurred.

If it's the last thing I do, Deputy Sheriff Ronald Jefferson thought bitterly, I'll pin it on the lying bastard. He won't get away with it — checking in at night, having this sidekick of his take his place during the night and coming back to Key West himself, having his sidekick check out in the morning (after eating the breakfast they'd agreed he'd eat), killing Dr. Piersal and — and laughing about it. Laughing at me. I'll —

And then, aloud, Deputy Sheriff Jefferson swore. You get mad, you let a little crook rile you, and you slip up. (Which is what the smart little crook is after.) It was a kind of sleight of hand. It was the old shell game.

Take the little crook back up again? (And listen to him talk about how pretty the water was.) Or . . .

XII

Pam suggested that, for this day, they pass up tennis. She said they didn't want to overdo it. She said she didn't have a muscle that wasn't furious at her. She said they could just loaf. They could lie in the sun, on the beach or at the pool, and work on tanning. Neither of them was really getting a tan. They'd get back home and nobody'd know they'd been in Florida.

Jerry thought this last was as unlike Pam North as anything he could think of. He thought, and said, that frying in oil was the last thing he would do voluntarily. He said, "Shuffleboard?" and Pam said, "For heaven's sake, Jerry!" in marked horror. Then Pam said she knew. They'd just drive around Key West. They would go down and watch the shrimp boats come in. They would have lunch at the A. & B. Lobster House. Or at this place near the Aquarium poor Dr. Piersal had mentioned. Or . . .

Key West is a small city on a small island. At its center — in the vicinity of Duval Street — traffic is thick and sluggish and there is no place to park, if one wants to park. Streets which promise well end disconcertingly nowhere, and with no room to turn around in.

"We could," Jerry said, "just sit here in the shade. When the *Times* gets here, we could read the *Times*. You could do the crossword."

"We'll go just as we are," Pam said. "If you've got your billfold."

Jerry had his billfold. They went just as they were, with Jerry's billfold in the pocket of his walking shorts and a large question mark in his mind.

At Pam's suggestion, they drove first up Roosevelt Boulevard, with the Atlantic sparkling on their right, with, far away, a tanker seemingly motionless in blue water. They passed the Martello Tower, which was a fortification once and is now a museum and art gallery; they passed the International Airport, which has not, since Castro, been particularly international. "Let's turn in here," Pam said, beyond the airport. "See what it looks like."

They could see, without turning in, what the Key Wester looked like. It looked like an affluent two-story motel, with "villas." Its grounds were thick with youngish palms, and bougainvillia brightly climbed the one-story office structure. Jerry turned the rented convertible, which they had converted, into the entrance and stopped it under the portico at the office door. Pam said she wouldn't be a minute, and was only three. That gave

Jerry time enough.

"Not there?" he said, when Pam was beside him.

"No," Pam said. "And hasn't been."

"A friend you're sure is in Key West somewhere, but you don't know where?"

"She wrote and told me," Pam said. "But I lost the letter. And we're leaving tomorrow and I do want to say hello before we have to say good-bye. They were very nice about it. Sorry she wasn't. Let's see what this one's like."

The Key Ambassador was like an affluent two-story motel, without villas, but with screened porches and a large swimming pool in the front yard. Mrs. Peter Coleman was not registered at the Key Ambassador, and had not been. Mrs. Coleman had also not been at the Howard Johnson Lodge or at Holiday House.

"There are," Jerry said, "probably a hundred motels in Key West. We told Jefferson about Mrs. Coleman. Anyway, it's a pretty wild — "

"I know," Pam said. "But Sheriff Jefferson has sold himself. On this Mr. Worthington. He doesn't really want any new theories."

"This one being precisely — where the hell do you think you're going?"

The last was to a fellow motorist, who also was going downtown on Roosevelt Boulevard, which was about to become Truman Avenue. Pam ignored it, as did the fellow motorist.

"Either," Pam said, "she actually saw her mother kill Dr. Piersal or found his body and knew her mother was here and put two and two together. So she got hold of mother and took her to Miami and put her on a train. Or a bus. Not an airplane, because then you give names. And, of course, got her hair done so this beachboy-waiter wouldn't recognize her. And found us last night so she could try out her story about driving up to Miami to get away from it all to see how it went over. And to be very surprised that Dr. Piersal was dead, of course. I thought for a moment, by the way, you were going to scare her off. Because you almost pointed out she had wondered *who* killed him, when she wasn't supposed to know anybody had, and an accident is always more likely."

Jerry said, "Oh."

Roosevelt Boulevard became Truman Avenue and narrowed and they crept in traffic, the sun beating on them, the air barely stirring. "Convertibles always *seem* like such a nice idea," Pam said, and at the next red light Jerry put the top up. They turned left in Simonton, toward a place where motels nestle, offering private beaches or beach privileges.

They found a place to park. "You take some and I'll take some," Pam suggested, and they went about it, Jerry feeling a good deal like a door-to-door salesman, peddling somewhat spurious merchandise. He also felt that they were both chasing a wild goose.

The luck was Pam's, as was proper. Jerry came out of the third motel which was sorry it had never heard of a Mrs. Peter Coleman — although it had had a Mrs. Roger Coleman in January — and Pam was waiting.

"There's where she was," Pam said, and pointed across the street.

"There" was "The Bougainvillia," with the flowers to prove it. Into The Bougainvillia Mrs. Peter Coleman had checked Friday, shortly after the arrival of the morning plane from Miami. Out of it she had checked Sunday morning, at a little after nine.

Pam had said how sorry she was to have missed her old friend and had expressed the hope, against hope, that it might be another Mrs. Peter Coleman; had said, "Dark hair? Not quite as tall as I am? Maybe asked about the greyhound races at Stock Island?" The Mrs. Coleman who had left Sunday morning — "although we'd thought she planned to stay on until the middle of the week" — was as described. And Friday night she had asked about the dog races, and got a cab to take her to them.

Pam hoped Deputy Sheriff Jefferson wouldn't be too sold on this Worthington-something to listen. They drove toward the county building to give him a chance.

Dr. Ferdinand Meister sounded testy on the telephone. He usually sounded testy, on the telephone or face to face.

He said, "This Upton cadaver. What were you looking for?"

Deputy Sheriff Jefferson said, "Cause of death, doctor."

He was asked if he had any idea what a long, dull, messy operation a thorough post-mortem is? He was told that, from what Dr. Meister knew of the history, a thoroughly competent man had already told him the cause of death. Jefferson said he was sorry, doctor. He almost said that he had called up to tell them they could forget about the autopsy, but managed not to say it. That wouldn't improve Dr. Meister's temper.

"All right," Dr. Meister said, "she died of heart disease. Of some standing, apparently. Her heart was hypertrophied. There was a subendocardial hemorrhage on the left side of the interventricular septum. Follow me?"

Dr. Meister knows damn well I don't follow him, Jefferson thought. He said, "Near enough, I guess. It was her heart, then?"

Dr. Meister snorted. He wanted to know what Jefferson thought he had just been saying. Jefferson said, "I'm sorry, doctor."

"In addition," Dr. Meister said, "she was a diabetic. She'd been taking insulin for that. She'd been taking digitalis for her heart — tablets. Found fragments in the stomach. She had arthritis, too. Had damn near everything people can have, the poor old girl."

The number of things people can have, and that medicine can't stop, was what made Dr. Ferdinand Meister testy. Jefferson knew that; everybody who knew Dr. Meister knew that. At moments, Dr. Meister even knew it himself.

"Anything wrong with her stomach?" Jefferson asked.

"No," Meister said. "Gastrointestinal tract pretty well normal. About the only thing in her that was, poor old girl. Liver — I can't say much for her liver. Wouldn't have cared to have had her gall bladder myself. Why? About her stomach?"

Jefferson told Dr. Meister about Mrs. Upton's upset stomach, about Dr. Piersal's treatment of it; about the intravenous injection that Dr. Upton thought probably had been of an anticonvulsant.

"Dramamine, probably," Meister said.

"Very quieting stuff, you know. Enough of it, and you go to sleep."

"Permanently?"

"Son," Dr. Meister said, "enough of damn near anything will put you to sleep permanently. Sure, I suppose Dramamine would. Never heard of its being used that way, but probably it would. So would too much insulin. So would too much digitalis, come to that. Or alcohol or . . ." He paused. "You say her stomach was upset?"

"Yes. That's what I hear."

"Bad?"

Jefferson gathered it had been pretty bad. Bad enough for her to call in a doctor. He said, "You mean she'd been drinking too much?"

Meister said, "What?" He said, "For God's sake, son. No — no alcohol in the blood. There's this — an overdose of digitalis makes people sick at the stomach. Very sick. Usually throw it up before it does any real harm — before it kills them. But it can make them pretty damn sick, son. If she took too many tablets . . ." He did not finish. Jefferson waited. He said, finally, "Just what is digitalis, doctor?"

"Glucoside," Dr. Meister said, helping Jefferson very little. "Powdered leaves of foxglove. Heart stimulant. Get somebody with rhythm disturbance and digitalis slows the beat down and strengthens it. Too much, and it slows it too much. Also you get nausea and thirsty as hell and maybe delirious. Maybe you even die. Not many do, because they throw it up. Get diarrhea, too. Still — people have died of it."

"Taking too many tablets?"

"Could be," Meister said. "People have killed themselves that way. Doing it a hard way."

"Could Mrs. Upton — "

"Now, son," Dr. Meister said, "how the hell would I know? She was taking digitalis, which was indicated for her heart condition. If she hadn't had a bad heart, and I found digitalis — well, I'd wonder like hell. But she did have. So — the autopsy shows she died of heart disease, with a hell of a lot of complications." He paused. "One hell of a lot," he said, sadly.

He was wasting time, Jefferson thought. He had his man; had him locked up. Still, there was no point in letting contrary theories float around loose.

"Doctor," he said, "if you'd treated her — when she was sick at her stomach, I mean — would you have wondered about digitalis?"

"She had a history of this sort of upset?" Meister said. "Gastrointestinal upset? Nervous indigestion?"

"Her husband says so."

"Then I doubt very much I'd have gone beyond that. Or that any doctor would."

"Dr. Piersal?"

"Look, son," Meister said. "I wasn't there. Remember? I don't know what he found, except that she was sick. He was one of the best internal medicine men in the country, and if he'd suspected anything else he'd have taken steps. Seems he just treated symptoms. So, it looked to him like a nervous stomach. So, about a thousand to one, that was what it was."

For that, Jefferson was entirely willing to settle. He considered. "I've got things to do, son," Meister said.

"Insulin," Jefferson said. "You said too much — "

"Son," Meister said, with great patience, "the poor old girl died of heart disease. If she took too much digitalis too, it can't be proved by autopsy. But I can tell you this — she didn't die of insulin shock. Normal glucose value in the blood. Normal for her condition, anyway. She was about due for another shot, in fact. She needed a couple of shots a day, I'd guess. So, son?"

Jefferson said, "Thanks, doctor. Sorry to have wasted your time."

"Oh," Dr. Meister said, "that seems to be

what it's for, son."

Jefferson hung up. He looked at his watch. Deputy Williams drove like a bat out of hell. Jefferson decided he'd go down and see what luck the boys had had in rounding up half a dozen thinnish men with narrow shoulders who were not markedly disfigured in any way and who had shaved recently.

Pam and Jerry North arrived five minutes after he had left his office. They left a message to the effect that Mrs. Peter Coleman, who had certainly had a grudge against Dr. Edmund Piersal, had been in Key West at least until nine o'clock Sunday morning, and that she had, apparently, left town sooner than she had first planned.

Miss Phyllis Farmer was a pretty little thing, in a fluffy sort of way. She said, "But goodness, I'm *on* at lunch."

Deputy Sheriff Williams had fixed that up with Mr. Hunter. He said he had fixed that up with Mr. Hunter. She said, "Oh, that," dismissing that. She said he apparently didn't realize that a girl had to make a living. She said that the season was short enough as it was, and another thing he didn't realize was that Hunter's Lodge wasn't American plan. With American plan it was one thing, because they didn't really pay any attention if a girl was off for a meal or two, but with European plan it was another. If you weren't there, you were out of luck.

Williams considered this briefly and said, "Oh. You're thinking about tips."

She had blue eyes. She widened them in astonishment. She said, what did he think she was talking about, for heaven's sake?

Williams said that maybe they could make it up to her, and that anyway he'd see, personally, that she had her own lunch on the county. She said that lunch didn't cost her anything here, for heaven's sake, and that anyway it didn't matter one way or another, because she always ate like a bird and usually just passed up lunch. She said it might come to six or seven dollars, and that a girl had to live.

Williams was considerably inclined to tell her to come off it, because six or seven dollars came to quite a lot of quarters, and that was what they tipped in — quarters. At lunch, anyway. On the other hand, he couldn't make her ride down to Key West, short of arresting her, which had not been suggested, and she looked like a girl who could get her back up — like a girl who knew her rights.

"I guess the county could go to five bucks," he said, sticking his neck out.

"I can't go like this," Miss Phyllis Farmer

said, looking at herself. She wore a white dress and white shoes, as a waitress should. "For heaven's *sake*," she added.

He waited while she changed. She changed to tapered slacks, which was all right with Williams, in view of her legs, and a blouse and a white sweater with sequins on it. She also put a red scarf over her blond hair. On the Seven Mile Bridge she said, "You certainly drive fast, for heaven's sake," but in a tone of approval. On Stock Island, she said, "Has this thing got a siren?" He proved it had. She said, "For heaven's *sake*."

"This is Miss Farmer," Williams told Chief Deputy Jefferson at the office. "She's the one. Says she doesn't know whether she can or not."

"One of them is just like another," Phyllis said. "You know how it is." Williams waited, expectant. "For heaven's sake," Phyllis added, faithful in her fashion.

Jefferson did understand. The man had, he thought, had breakfast alone. She had served him. The check proved that — after the printed "Your waitress is: " she had written "Phyllis." Williams had brought the check along and they showed it to her. She said of course that was her name. She looked at the slip more carefully. She said, "Maybe I can, at that."

The boys had been able to round up only

four men of the requested size and shape. They did not look much alike. On the other hand, they did not look too much un-alike. Worthington-Bradley made five, and they put him in the middle. The whole business seemed to amuse him, mildly.

The girl looked at them carefully, one by one. It seemed to Jefferson, watching, that she looked longest at Jasper Bradley. His hope diminished. But she looked for some time, too, at the man at the end of the line. Then she turned to Jefferson, and then she shook her brightly scarfed head.

"It wasn't any one of them, for heaven's sake," Miss Phyllis Farmer said, and Ronald Jefferson's spirits jumped.

"I'm sorry," the girl said.

"That's all right," Jefferson told her. There was no point in stressing just how all right it was. "You're sure, though?"

"Of course I'm sure," the girl said. "As soon as I looked at the check I remembered. When they make trouble you look at them." She seemed to feel this incomplete. She completed it. "For heaven's sake."

Jefferson said, "Trouble?"

"Right there on the check," she said, "it says soft. It's underlined. 'Scrambled eggs soft.' And I told the chef for heaven's sake, and he sent them back because they were too

194

hard. So I knew he was one of the fussy ones and I looked at him so that the next time I could maybe steer him to Harriet's table. Only, he didn't come back. So I know he's not there."

She gestured toward the five men, still standing in a row, and Jefferson looked, and he was quick enough.

Jasper Bradley did not look amused. He looked, Jefferson thought, mad as hell, and he could guess who Bradley was mad at. His sidekick had loused it up. His sidekick should have eaten, inconspicuously, what they had agreed should be put before him. If Bradley caught up with his sidekick — man named Ashley, hundred to one — he'd make him eat hard-cooked eggs until they came out of his ears. But it wasn't likely Bradley would be in a position to catch up with anyone.

Jefferson decided to let Bradley stew in it for a while, and had him sent back to his cell. He told Deputy Williams to take Miss Farmer somewhere and buy her a nice lunch on the county. Miss Farmer looked at Williams fixedly.

"I sort of told her," Williams said, "that we'd make up to her what tips she lost by not working this noon."

"Sort of like how much?" Jefferson said, and Williams told him.

"Go right ahead," Jefferson said. Williams said, "Now listen, Jeff — "

"O.K.," Jefferson said. "Make out a voucher for it and the lunch. I'll try to get it by the old man."

There were a number of papers in Jefferson's "In" basket. He decided to let them go until after lunch. He figured he had earned a break. He also figured he had earned a good lunch, and left word that he would be at the A. & B. Lobster House, if wanted.

XIII

The A. & B. Lobster House is a large restaurant, largely surrounded by water. From its windows one can look down on shrimp boats and count the hopeful cats waiting at the dock. But, large as it is, the restaurant was crowded that Monday noon. Pam and Jerry waited at the bar for a table. They had said it had better be for three, since a friend might join them.

"Chances are," Jerry said, as they waited for the barman to work to them, "he's too hipped on this fellow Bradley to waste time on anything else."

Pam was watching the barman, and merely nodded her head. The barman had filled a glass with ice, and poured a jigger of vodka into it, and now was pouring, over the vodka, a dark brown fluid from a little jug. When he had filled the glass, he squeezed half a lime over it, and dropped the squeezed lime in.

"What," Pam said, "is that? The brown stuff?"

"Beef bouillon," the barman told her. "And vodka and lime juice."

"I'll have one," Pam said, and made acquaintance with the drink known, somewhat

197

perilously, as a "bull shot." She reported it very good, and probably nourishing. "Extra-dry martini," Jerry told the barman. "House of Lords."

"Got Beefeater," the barman said.

"Beefeater," Jerry said.

"He'll be interested," Pam said. "See, I told you he would."

From their stools they could see the door. Deputy Sheriff Ronald Jefferson had appeared in it. "Over here," Pam said, using just as much voice as she needed, and adding, "Mr. Jefferson."

Jefferson came to join them.

"I was just telling Jerry you'd be interested," Pam said.

Jefferson looked entirely blank.

"In Mrs. Coleman."

Jefferson shook his head.

"We left a message," Jerry said. "About her. And that we'd be here."

Jefferson said he had had a busy morning. "Bourbon and plain water, Sam." He said, "Looks like we've got Bradley where we want him." He sipped. "What about Mrs. Coleman?"

They told him about Mrs. Coleman, complete with theory. They showed him Bill Weigand's telegram. He said it was pretty interesting, but didn't, to Pam, sound particularly interested. He said that, even if it was the right Mrs. Coleman, it didn't have to mean what they thought it meant.

"This is the way it is. We've got a man with a good motive — hell of a lot better motive than this Mrs. Coleman would have. Also, he rigs up a phoney alibi to cover the right time — just the right time. Here's what we've got on — "

They were told their table was ready. They picked up their drinks and walked.

" — that," Jefferson said, when they were at the table, and told them about that. He said that if Bradley's sidekick hadn't been so particular about the way he got his eggs, Bradley might have got away with it. He said they'd notice that the time Bradley wanted to cover was almost precisely the time Dr. Piersal was killed.

"We've got him cold, the crooked — " Jefferson said, and checked himself, there being a lady present. But he made no effort to keep out of his voice a note of satisfaction which amounted almost to triumph. "And he knows it. You could see that by looking at him. Wouldn't be surprised if, after he thinks it over a while, he doesn't come clean. Particularly as he can involve this sidekick, who loused things up for him."

He looked to the Norths for approval. They nodded their heads appropriately.

"Of course," he said, "I'll check it out about Mrs. Coleman. If her daughter did pick her up and take her to Miami, I'll check that out with her daughter."

He doesn't, Pam thought, want us to feel unappreciated. "Sure," Jerry said. "But probably you're right."

"One thing we can wash out," Jefferson said. "The idea that Dr. Piersal made some mistake in treating Mrs. Upton. Doc Meister did an autopsy this morning and — "

He told them of the findings. He's a nice young man, Pam thought. He's telling us all this so we won't feel left out, frustrated. But she also listened to Jefferson's summary of the pathologist's findings.

"So you see it doesn't tie in," Jefferson said, when he had finished. "She died of a heart attack. I don't suppose being as sick as she was did her heart any good, but it was the heart killed her. There's the digitalis angle, so could be there's a chance she just got fed up with being sick all the time and — well, there the stuff was, handy. If she hadn't been taking it and it showed up in — in the remains, it would look pretty fishy. But she had been taking it."

It was apparent that the death of Mrs. Tucker Upton had no connection with that of Dr. Edmund Piersal; that it was one of those coincidences which are so troublesome in the investigation of crime. Jerry said, "Insulin?" and Jefferson went over that again. She'd been on insulin; probably had needed two injections a day. Her husband had given her one Saturday morning before he went to Miami. Presumably she had given herself the second shot some time Saturday evening. Her husband had said she hated to do it, but when she had to, she could nerve herself to it.

"It was," Pam said, "just a theory. I never did think much of it, really. Probably it's the way you think, this Worthington-Bradley man."

Jerry could tell from Pam's tone that she was a little disappointed; that she considered this Worthington-Bradley man somewhat anticlimactic. He did not share her disappointment. If it was all wound up, and wound around Worthington-Bradley, they could return to holiday, which had been interrupted by pelicans, with murder superimposed. It was true that Mrs. Coleman remained, but —

The waitress came. Pam was saying, "Yellow tail, please," when the hostess came to tell Chief Deputy Sheriff Ronald Jefferson that he was wanted on the telephone. Jefferson said, "Damn it," swallowed the rest of his drink and went. Jerry said, "Pompano," and the waitress said of course, if he didn't mind waiting a little longer, because the pompano was frozen. "Yellow tail," Jerry said. "Anyway, either will take quite a little time, won't it?"

"We cook everything to order," the waitress said.

Jerry looked at their empty glasses. He looked at Pam. She guessed so, only a martini this time — a vodka martini. Jerry stuck to Beefeater. Pam said that policemen were always missing meals, the poor things.

"Probably," Jerry said, "this Bradley guy has decided to come clean."

"I still think — " Pam said, and did not continue. She had stopped, Jerry thought, to turn her mind over, because she had noticed something under it. He waited.

"It's all right," Pam said. "I just remembered something, I think."

"That thing that was on the tip of your mind?"

She considered that. She said, "I don't think so. This is about the dogs. The other must have been about something else, because the dogs just came up."

Jerry nodded his head. The tip of Pam's mind had had something on it before the matter of dog races came up.

"She asked about them," Pam said. "And got a taxi to go to them. That was Friday night, they said. And Dr. Piersal was there the same night. Remember? He told us that, if we'd never seen a dog race, we might enjoy it. That he'd been the night before. That was Saturday, when we were having drinks at the pool bar. She might have seen him there."

There might well, Jerry pointed out, have been hundreds of people there. Thousands, for all he knew.

"They bet at them, don't they?" Pam said, and Jerry said that was the main point, usually. "At those something windows," Pam said. "It would — channel them, wouldn't it? I mean, like through a funnel?"

"It might."

"She may have come down here quite innocently," she said. "Not knowing the doctor was here. Then she saw him and — and it all came back. All the hatred, I mean. So . . ." She looked at Jerry and now it was she who waited.

"She got a knife," Jerry said. "Knew he would be out at the end of the pier at seven o'clock Sunday morning. Followed him out and he, who was a big man and a strong one, let her — and she weighs a hundred and twenty and's five feet four — let her . . ."

"I know," Pam said. "There are holes in it. Here come our drinks."

Chief Deputy Sheriff Ronald Jefferson tried

203

not to believe it. But there it was, in a chair at the end of his desk, and mad as mad could be. With cause, Jefferson began to be afraid, and his spirits sank. The crooked little so-and-so, Jefferson thought.

The man at the end of the desk, and mad as a man could be, was not the crooked little so-and-so. He was William Howard Alexander. He was not especially little; was inclined to corpulence. He was also inclined to be red in the face, partly from sunburn and partly from anger. He was not a man used to being arrested.

He had been arrested — not by the sheriff's men; there was that — when he took a fishing boat in to a dock on Stock Island and tied it up, and got out of it with his day's catch, which was satisfactory. He had been arrested by the state police who, with the aid of the Coast Guard, had been looking for him since mid-morning. He was arrested just after dark Sunday evening. He was arrested, since the fishing boat was not his boat, on the charge of stealing it.

A Coast Guard cutter had picked up the boat — which was called the *Amy Lou* — some distance out in the Gulf but, since it seemed to be heading home, had merely trailed it in. The police were waiting its arrival, along with Captain Mark Dobie, to whom it belonged.

When he was told to come along, now, the large and corpulent man appeared at first astonished, and then, almost instantly, enraged.

He asked the state troopers, rather unnecessarily, who the hell they thought they were and then, perhaps more reasonably, who the hell they thought *he* was. Captain Dobie had an answer to that one: "You're the s.o.b. who stole my boat." The corpulent man had one word for that. He then said, "You don't know who I am," which was at that moment entirely true. He then told them that they'd damn soon find out who he was. Policemen all over the world are familiar with this approach, and tired of it.

"I'm William Howard Alexander," the corpulent man said, taking care of that part of it. He then, it appeared, waited for gasps of amazement.

The state police sergeant in charge said, "So what, mister?"

This seemed to amaze William Howard Alexander, who repeated his name, slowly and carefully and expectantly. When the sergeant said, "So all right, you're William Howard Alexander. You expect a band or something?" Alexander promptly blew up again. It then became apparent that he had had several drinks, as a man may well have in a day's fishing. He didn't, he said, know who this little runt was — Captain Dobie wasn't a large man, but he was well-seasoned — or what the hell this was all about, but he'd bought the boat and no lousy little . . . He went on on this course for several minutes before Dobie hit him, with considerable violence, in the most prominent target, his belly.

They locked William Howard Alexander up at this point, although he told them they'd find out, soon enough, who he was.

They hadn't, not soon enough. His attitude did not move them to haste, and Sunday night is a bad night to find things out in.

It had not been until almost ten Monday morning that a state police lieutenant looked at a message from Miami, and said, "Ouch," and summoned the sergeant to ask him what the hell he thought he had been up to.

William Howard Alexander was Alexander Enterprises, Inc., and he had, among other things, just bought one of the most flamboyant hotels on Miami Beach. He was in Key West to decide whether he wanted to add The Coral Isles to his chain and his office in Miami — he had offices almost everywhere — had been trying to get in touch with him to report that the Belmoth Shipping Corporation had come through with a counter proposal, asking only a million more than Alexander Enterprises had offered for the fleet. They unlocked Mr.

Alexander, who was not noticeably mollified by a night in jail. In the course of refusing to accept their apologies, and between references to a suit for false arrest, he happened to mention "a man said his name was Worthington."

It was then that the Deputy Sheriff's lunch was interrupted.

Jefferson told William Howard Alexander that he, along with everybody else, was sorry as hell. Alexander said he, and everybody else, damned well should be, and what had they thought he brought the boat back for, if he'd stolen it? It was, Jefferson agreed, a point which certainly should have occurred to somebody. He knew it was an imposition, but would Mr. Alexander mind going over it again? Alexander spluttered, and said he damned well would mind. But after a time he did go over it again.

He had come down to do a week's fishing and decided to "pick up a boat." He spoke of this, Jefferson thought, as another man might speak of picking up a handkerchief. He had mentioned his purpose aloud — and what William Howard Alexander said aloud could be widely heard — while he was having a drink somewhere, and this man said his name was Worthington had come over and said he couldn't help overhearing, and that he had a boat he'd sell cheap. This had been Saturday afternoon some time.

"Looked all right," Alexander said. "Had a yachting cap on."

The man had driven him over to Stock Island and showed him the *Amy Lou,* and it wasn't much, but looked all right, and the man didn't want much for it. The man who said his name was Worthington said he'd take Mr. Alexander out for a run in her, only she wasn't gassed up. He said he'd have her ready the next morning and that Mr. Alexander could then, if he wanted, take her out for the day and try her. He didn't want Mr. Alexander to feel he was buying a pig in a poke. All he'd ask down would be what you could call an option payment. Maybe five hundred.

"Couldn't quarrel with that," Alexander said. "He said he couldn't go himself and show me, because he had a charter in his other boat, and that if I didn't like the boat he'd return the five hundred, less what the gas cost. So I met him yesterday morning — "

"What time?" Jefferson asked, and was afraid he knew.

"Seven o'clock."

Jefferson had known, all right.

"You paid him cash?"

Alexander looked slightly surprised, and said, "Sure." The implication was, Ronald

Jefferson thought, that a man didn't use a check to pay so trivial a sum — hardly more than bus fare, really.

Alexander had got a receipt and chugged off in the *Amy Lou*.

"Keys?"

"Sure he gave me the keys."

"They fitted?"

Jefferson knew the question was silly; Mr. William Howard Alexander had spent the day chugging around the Gulf in the boat. Alexander answered with what Jefferson took to be an affirmative snort. Alexander was still very sore about the whole business, and couldn't be blamed for that. He was probably, Jefferson thought, as sore at himself as at any one else, and he had cause for that, too. He'd been a prize sucker.

"He's a plausible bastard," Alexander said, giving himself that much. Asked, he showed Jefferson the receipt — a receipt for five hundred dollars ($500) accepted as option payment on the boat *Amy Lou*, to be refunded, less cost of gas and of any repairs which might be necessary, if William Howard Alexander was not satisfied after a one-day trial run. The receipt, which Jefferson had to admit sounded fine, sounded businesslike, was signed "James Worthington."

Jefferson had Worthington-Bradley brought

in then. The narrow-shouldered man looked at Alexander blankly. Alexander did not look blank at all. He said, "That's the son of bitch."

At this, Bradley looked pained; looked with pain from the florid and corpulent man to Deputy Sheriff Jefferson. He sighed. The little so-and-so was a great one for sighing.

"I'm afraid I don't know this gentleman," Bradley said.

"You're a lying bastard," Alexander said. "You got five hundred of my money."

Bradley looked at Jefferson and raised his eyebrows.

"This gentleman," Jefferson said, and kept his voice even, although it was an effort, "charges that you accepted five hundred dollars from him as a down payment on a boat you didn't own."

"Does he?" Bradley said. "When was this — er — fraudulent transaction supposed to have taken place?"

"Seven o'clock yesterday morning," Alexander said. "As you know damn well."

Bradley sighed again — sighed his patient, tolerant sigh. Briefly, Jefferson thought of wiping up the floor with him.

"I was in Marathon at that hour," Bradley said, and his voice was patient. "I'm afraid it's mistaken identity, sir."

He was going to stick to it. Jefferson wasn't

surprised. He and Ashley, or whatever the sidekick's name really was, had gone to a spot of trouble, and some expense, to set up an alibi for a minor swindle. It would be Bradley's word against that of a fluffy little waitress. His word, his fingerprints and, of course, Lem Hunter's identification. Still, he'd probably lose in the end, and Monroe County probably would get a bite at him, if Dade County left anything unbitten.

The alibi might have been good enough for a minor swindle. Murder is a different matter; it wasn't good enough for murder.

The little so-and-so didn't need it for that. Not any more. For that Mr. William Howard Alexander had just given him all the alibi any man could need.

Jefferson arranged for Alexander to file his complaint, and for Bradley to be put back in his cell. He returned to his desk and sat at it glumly.

The bottom had fallen out. Jefferson felt that he had fallen out with it. He sighed. He would have to start the way the Norths had pointed, which probably would be up another blind alley. The Upton angle — that had been a blind alley. The Bradley angle — that had been another, although it had seemed to open up like Roosevelt Boulevard.

Deputy Sheriff Jefferson got his car and

drove on Simonton Street until he was almost at its end. He parked and went into the motel — the new and glossy resort motel known as "The Bougainvillia." He said, "Afternoon, Norma," to the glossy young woman behind the desk.

"If," she said, "it isn't the sheriff."

He said there was, anyway had been, a Mrs. Coleman, Mrs. Peter Coleman.

"Left Sunday morning, Jeff," Norma Still said, promptly. "Reason I know, somebody else was asking. Just a couple of hours ago. What's about this Mrs. Coleman?"

Jefferson had got himself ready for that.

"Seems her daughter's worrying about her," he said. "Seems she's in bad health. And sort of — well, eccentric's the word for it, I guess. Her daughter's worried about her. Asked us to check up, see if she was all right. Asked the city police first, but they turned it over to us. Like always."

"The woman who asked earlier," Norma Still said, "said Mrs. Coleman was a friend of hers. Knew she was in Key West, but had lost the letter Mrs. Coleman wrote saying where. Younger than Mrs. Coleman, but not that much younger. I mean not to be her daughter."

"Just a coincidence, I guess," Jefferson said. "What I wonder whether you can tell me — "

Checked in Friday, expecting to stay about a week. Checked out Sunday, at about nine in the morning. She had not telephoned anybody Sunday morning before she left. There would have been a record of that. Whether anybody had called her she couldn't say. No record of incoming calls. Of course, Doris might happen to remember —

She went; she returned. Doris, at the switchboard, did happen to remember. If it hadn't been so early, particularly on Sunday morning, she wouldn't have. But at that hour there weren't many calls. She was pretty sure somebody had called Mrs. Coleman. She thought at about eight.

Ronald Jefferson felt, then, less like a man merely going through motions.

Doris thought, further, that it was a woman who had called. She was, however, much less certain about this.

Norma Still had been on the desk when Mrs. Coleman arrived on Friday. It had been at about the time she would have got there if she had flown in to Miami on the morning plane. She wore the dark, wintry clothing fliers from New York to Florida have no time to change. And — Norma interrupted herself to snap her fingers. She had come by taxi. The taxi man had carried her bags into the office, and waited until he was sure there was a room available.

"But if she'd gone by taxi, Jeff, she'd have had to call one. And there'd have been a record."

Jefferson had long considered Norma Still a bright girl, as well as a pretty one. He felt his judgment confirmed.

"And," Norma said, proving it further, "she had a room on the second floor so — " She looked toward the standup desk at which a youth in walking shorts and white stockings, and a white uniform jacket with green facings, waited for something to happen. She said, "Joady!"

Joady came. Joady said, let's see, that would be Jimmy and Jimmy was just showing No. 135 where to park and ought — "Here he is now."

Jimmy, a redheaded young man in walking shorts and white stockings and white jacket faced with green, did remember. He had helped No. 117 down with her bags and put them in her car for her. Well, he supposed it was her car. It was in 117's slot. Yes — wait a minute.

Jefferson waited less than a minute. Jimmy snapped his fingers. There had already been a woman in the car, behind the wheel. A young woman, with black hair — sort of lanky black hair, if the sheriff knew what he meant. He hadn't noticed what she'd been wearing. Maybe a suit of some sort. No, not white shorts and a blue jacket. He'd have noticed if she'd been wearing shorts. Suit of some sort, or maybe a dress. The car? The car was a Chevy Bel Air, two-tone green. It was a rental. From the Key West office. "They put numbers on the license plates," Jimmy said. "There's a key digit shows the office."

Jefferson thanked everybody and drove to the Hertz rental office.

A Chevrolet Bel Air, two-tone green, had been checked out at 8:35 Sunday morning to Mrs. Rebecca Payne, local address The Coral Isles, New York driver's license, American Express credit card. The car had been returned at 6:47 Sunday evening, and Mrs. Payne had been driven to The Coral Isles. The car had been driven three hundred and forty-one miles. Mrs. Payne had expended, and been reimbursed, six dollars and forty-seven cents for gasoline.

The alley might still be blind. It was beginning to look a little wider than it had at first.

XIV

Pam was, she said, a little put out with Chief Deputy Sheriff Jefferson. He might at least have come back and told them that it was over; that Jasper Bradley had decided to tell all. He owed them that much, after the trouble he had put them to.

It was, Jerry pointed out, rather the other way round. "If you," he said, "hadn't got so pally with those damn birds."

"Somebody else would have," Pam said. "He — he wouldn't just have lain there. And we made several suggestions." She paused then. "Of course," she said, "they maybe weren't very good. Still . . ."

They were driving back to the hotel, then. They had somewhat dawdled over lunch, waiting for Jefferson to come back or, at the least, send a message back.

"And," Pam said, as they walked from parking lot to hotel entrance, "I don't like coincidences. Let's go look at the ocean."

Jerry had thought of a nap, but Pam is very fond of looking at oceans. They went through the hotel and, on the porch on the ocean side, Jerry said, "There's two," and nodded toward chairs. The ocean was in plain view from ei-

216

ther. The Atlantic, at Key West, makes itself visible.

Pam was, by then, going down the steps, out into the sun. Jerry followed her; when Pam wishes to look at an ocean she prefers a front seat. They walked down the pathway which led to a tall evergreen hedge, with a gap in it, and the ocean beyond. They went through the gap, past comfortable chaises in its shade, and sat side by side on a bench (which was not especially comfortable) in the sun. The ocean was still some yards away, across a lumpy coral beach. The Atlantic was not particularly restless; the ocean murmured, did not roar. But the Atlantic, at its most reserved, murmurs loudly.

Ships moved on it, and seemed to be heading away, but were not — were rounding the island toward the naval base. A cruiser and two destroyers, Jerry thought. And — yes, ahead of them the submarine they had spent most of the day chasing. Almost every day surface ships and submarines play hide and seek off Key West.

"I wish we wouldn't," Pam said. "I wish nobody would. I feel the same way about the moon, as a matter of fact. Somebody's cow flies over it first, and so what? Lands on it, and so what?"

"Man's instinct to explore," Jerry said. He

did not say it with any special conviction. One uses worn phrases in lieu of something better. It was warm in the sun; one grew drowsy in the sun. They could start worrying again in a brisker —

"In the almost hurricane last fall," Pam said, "that — " she gestured toward the Atlantic — "washed away hundreds of houses and things, and killed a lot of people. Where we live, or almost. South Jersey and Long Island and — why don't we use all that moon money to build a wall, or something?"

"I don't know."

"It must be simpler than flying to the moon," Pam said. "And back."

"Much," Jerry said. "We can't solve it, Pam. Not here. Not now."

There was a considerable pause.

"It isn't one of our better days, is it?" Pam said. "We can't solve the moon business. We find Mrs. Coleman and it is only a coincidence."

Jerry said, "What?" He flicked his hand toward the ocean. "Makes a noise," he said.

"Mrs. Coleman," Pam said, more loudly. "Her having a grudge against poor Dr. Piersal and being here and its not meaning — "

"How did you know that?" Rebecca Payne said, behind them. They turned. She was standing in the gap of the hedge — a slim,

218

dark girl in white shorts and a blue shirt. Jerry stood up. "She was — all right, she was. She had as much right to be here as — "

"Of course," Jerry said.

"As to how we knew," Pam said, "we went places and asked. Because a man was murdered." She paused a moment. "A very nice man," she said. "A man we'd played tennis with. Had drinks with."

"And," Rebecca said, with bitterness in her voice, "you jumped to things — absurd, vicious things."

"No," Pam said. "Wondered about things, Mrs. Payne. When you drove to Miami yesterday. Was it to take your mother away from here?"

"It's not your business," Rebecca Payne said.

"No," Jerry said. "It's not our business."

"But you — pried into it. I suppose — told this sheriff?"

"It's not a little thing," Jerry said, and spoke gently. "It's a man killed. A man who's done a lot of things for people. Who might have done more things. But, at bottom, a man killed. It doesn't really matter who he was."

"And," Pam said, "we have told the sheriff. And — he isn't much interested."

"There's no reason why — " the girl began, and there was still bitterness in her raised voice. But she stopped, as if she had just heard, and said, "Isn't interested?"

"Not much," Pam said. "He's got — he's pretty sure he has anyway — the man who killed Dr. Piersal."

The girl stood and looked at them.

"Yes," Pam said.

For an instant, the girl seemed to sway a little, standing there in the sun. She caught her breath, and the sound was almost that of a sob.

"I'm sorry I spoke that way," Rebecca Payne said. "I'm always having to say I'm sorry, aren't I? How did you know I took mother to Miami?" She looked at them, intently. "You didn't really, did you?" she said, and spoke to Pam.

"Only guessed," Pam said. "You did, then?"

"Before any of — " Rebecca began. "No, before I knew about any of this. About the doctor. She didn't know at all, of course. Oh, I suppose she does now. It's in the papers — the Miami papers."

Anyone who read newspapers, or watched television or listened to radio would know by now.

"Let's," Rebecca said, "go where it's shady. Where it isn't so noisy." She gestured toward the ocean. "You may as well know. Not that there's really anything to know."

They found a shady corner on the porch. She had not known, Rebecca told them, that her mother was in Key West. Not until Saturday. She had thought her still in the — she hesitated for a moment, and chose "rest home." But on Saturday, just before lunch, her mother had telephoned her, and said she was in Key West, and where in Key West.

"I was surprised," Rebecca said. "But — " She shrugged the slender shoulders under the dark blue shirt. "Frankly," she said, "mother's a bit of a problem. I don't mean just since this last — upset. She's — unpredictable. It's been that way ever since father died. It's — somehow it's as if she had — I don't know. Been cut loose? She used to be — used to plan things, the way other people do. Now it's all impulse. Coming down here was that."

"She knew you were here?"

"Of course. But she didn't come to be with me. She thinks — well, I suppose that people are trying to tell her what to do. That I am. And I am, I guess. She wants to go her own way."

"To this motel," Pam said. "Instead of here, to The Coral Isles."

"Of course," Rebecca said. "That was part of it. Don't you see?"

"Part of going her own way?"

Rebecca Payne said that of course that was it. But then she paused, and Jerry thought, She's going to explain herself again. He felt, as he had felt before, an odd amalgam of sympathy and irritation.

"I wanted it that way, too," she said. "She knew I did. It's — I'm trying to decide something. I want to be alone to think things out."

It was a cliché, Pam thought. And people live by clichés.

"Alone," Rebecca said, "or with strangers. People who are — outside. Not part of anything."

And, feeling this, Jerry thought — almost surely really feeling this — she is driven to bring people inside, make them part of her. As now, he thought, she is bringing us. Seeking to be alone; afraid of loneliness.

"Anyway," Rebecca said, "she called me Saturday. Said she was here and had planned to stay about a week, but now wasn't sure she would. Said she couldn't see what I saw in Key West; couldn't see what anybody saw. She — oh, she ran on. She does, sometimes. About — a good deal about — having been to the dog races the night before. Said they were dull, not like real races. She — well, she loves going to the tracks, betting at the tracks." She paused. She smiled faintly. "Probably lost money on the dogs," she said. "Anyway — "

They had arranged to lunch together Sunday. But Rebecca had not, she said, been surprised — not really surprised — when her mother called her up early Sunday morning and asked her to rent a car and drive her up to Miami. Mrs. Coleman did not herself drive; hadn't for years. There had been an accident. Rebecca did not know much about that; it had been when she was a little girl. As for a bus — "She'd never think of a bus. Buses are — oh, for a different kind of person. She's like that. Shuts out whole areas. Anyway — "

Anyway, driving to Miami fitted well enough with what Rebecca herself wanted. "I was upset about the day before," she said. "About the way I acted. That was true. I didn't say anything about mother because — well, you can see why I wouldn't."

They could.

Rebecca had rented a car and picked her mother up at, she thought, about nine o'clock. She hadn't, then, known anything about the murder. They had driven to Miami, and Mrs. Coleman had checked in at the Columbus. They had had lunch at the Columbus, in the roof restaurant — the "Top of the Columbus." From there they could see all Miami. After lunch, Mrs. Coleman had gone to her room. Rebecca had driven around Miami, as she had said before; along Collins Avenue on Miami Beach, as she had said before.

"And," Pam said, "got your hair done. And very well, too."

And got her hair done. And driven back and turned the car in. And found that the maid hadn't, even then, got around to doing her room.

"That," Rebecca said, "was all there was to it. When I got back and you told me about the poor doctor there wasn't any point in saying anything about mother's having been here. Raking up the past that hadn't anything to do with it. You can see that."

"Of course," Pam said.

And it was understandable. It was what anybody might do; it was the sort of thing which, in similar circumstances, people almost always did. In such extreme circumstances as these, it gave the police a good deal of extra trouble, but policemen are invented to be troubled. In this special case, of course, it was, Pam added, we who were troubled. Finding a coincidence without meaning, tracing it down and —

It was, Pam thought, a little as if Chief Deputy Sheriff Jefferson had been waiting in the wings. He made his entrance along the porch, to their shady corner. He looked very tall, and a little tired and hot, and remarkably unsmiling. He nodded to the Norths and stood and looked down at Rebecca Payne. He said, "Mrs. Payne. There are a few things I want to ask you." He paused for a moment. "About your mother," he said, rather heavily. "About your helping her get away." He paused again. "And," he said, "there's no point in your saying you didn't."

She looked up at him.

"To get away?" she said. "It wasn't to help her get away, as you put it. It was — "

She looked at Pam North. It was as if she turned to Pam for help.

"She's just been telling us about it," Pam said. And then, interrupting herself, "What's happened to this Mr. Bradley? I thought he . . ."

She left it there, in the air for Jefferson to field. Somewhat to her surprise, Jefferson looked at her angrily. His lips started to move, and Pam, no lip reader, was rather glad she wasn't. But then the expression of anger faded, and Jefferson said, "Sorry, Miz North," but did not say for what. She could guess. That Mr. Bradley had riled Jefferson.

"There's been a hitch," Jefferson said. "Anyway, we have to look into all possibilities."

"Apparently Mrs. Coleman isn't one," Pam said. "She just wanted to go to Miami. Her being here at all was just — " Pam hesitated, shunning a word. "Just happened to happen," Pam said. "So she called her daughter up and they drove up together. Neither of them knew what had happened."

"All right," Jefferson said. "She called you up, did she, Mrs. Payne?"

"Yes."

"When was this?"

"Yesterday morning," Rebecca said. "Quite early and — "

She stopped. Jefferson was slowly, with emphasis, shaking his head.

"Nope," he said. "I checked on that. She didn't make any calls. The motel switchboard keeps a record. No calls."

Pam, watching, could see the change in the dark girl's face. The change was a faint sagging of muscles, the faint look of defeat. Pam hoped she wasn't really seeing what she thought she saw.

"She did telephone me," Rebecca said, but her voice was dull. "Perhaps they made a mistake at the motel."

Jefferson shook his head again. "They charge for calls," he said. "They don't slip up on that sort of thing."

Anybody can slip up on almost anything, Pam thought. But —

"Then maybe," Rebecca said, "she called from some place else."

Jefferson had one word: "Why?"

It was, Pam thought, a very good word. She looked at Jerry and knew that he, too, thought it a good word. She had seen enough of The Bougainvillia to know that it was the sort of motel which has a telephone in every room. Mrs. Coleman would have had only to reach out toward a table by her bed —

"There's a telephone in the room," Jefferson said. "Why wouldn't she use that?"

Rebecca Payne looked again at Pam, but this time Pam could only, if unhappily, lift her shoulders.

"I don't know," Rebecca said. "She did — "

"No," Jefferson said. "I'm afraid not, Mrs. Payne. Did you call her?"

"That was it," Rebecca said. But she spoke too quickly. And again, Jefferson used the single word: "Why?

"To see if she was there?" he asked, when the dark girl merely looked at nothing, as if there were nothing anywhere to see. "Because you knew Dr. Piersal had been killed? Had gone out on the pier and found him dead. And knew your mother was in town and were afraid — "

"No," the girl said, "it wasn't that way. It — "

Then, suddenly, she covered her face with her hands.

After a time, she spoke from behind the covering hands, her voice muffled.

"She didn't have anything to do with it," she said. "She couldn't have. I know she — "

And then her shoulders began to shake. There was nothing to do but wait. It seemed to Pam that they waited a long time before Rebecca Payne took her hands down and said, "I'm sorry. I — " She paused again, and drew her breath in. "It wasn't quite the way I said," she told them. "It — " And then she stopped. Again they waited. It was Pam, finally, who spoke first.

"My dear," she said, "when your mother called you Saturday. Did she say she had seen Dr. Piersal at the greyhound races the night before? Was that why you were afraid?"

Slowly, as if she could not help herself, Rebecca Payne nodded her head.

"The boy?" she said, her voice dull. "The boy who takes care of the beach. He saw me? Is that it?"

"Yes," Jefferson said. "He saw you."

And had, Pam thought, been unable to identify her. But that didn't matter now.

"I was afraid he had," Rebecca said. "I had my hair done another way but — " She shrugged her shoulders, helplessly. "I went out there," she said. "I — I saw the doctor. And, yes, mother had mentioned seeing him at the track. And — "

It had been that — that her mother was in Key West, and knew that Dr. Piersal was in Key West — which had frightened her. She told them that, speaking slowly, choosing words carefully. She had been too worried, too upset, Saturday night to sleep well. Quite early in the morning she had given up trying to sleep at all. She had put on a bathing suit, and a jacket, and gone out. "To wash it away," she said. She had gone out on the pier toward the steps which led down to the screened water enclosure, and, when she was at the head of the steps, had looked up the pier and seen someone lying on the board flooring. "There was something about the way he was lying that didn't look — looked unnatural."

She had walked toward the man lying on the pier, and seen the blood and known who he was and that he was dead.

He might not have been, Jefferson thought. A layman can't be sure. But it wouldn't have made any difference. And there was no point, now, in interrupting her.

Her one thought, then, had been to get to her mother, to find out whether her mother was at the motel or — She did not finish that.

Her first plan had been to go back to her room and telephone her mother. But she had seen the beachboy and thought he had seen her, but was not sure, and hoped that, if he had, he would not recognize her. So, when she saw the gate which opened on Flagler Avenue was ajar, she had gone that way.

She had known where the motel was; her mother had told her that, and that it was only a few blocks from The Coral Isles. She also knew the number of her mother's room — she had learned that when they had arranged to meet for lunch — and that it could be reached, as can most motel rooms, without going through the lobby. She had climbed the stairs and found the room and knocked.

"And," Rebecca said, "she was there. I — I waked her up. So I knew that — that what I had been afraid of — that it couldn't be true. That she couldn't have — have been there and — and have got back and been asleep and — "

She edges around it, Pam thought. Which is natural. You think your mother has killed someone and find she hasn't, can't have —

"You told her about Dr. Piersal," Jefferson said.

"Yes. And we both decided that it would be better if she — well, if she went to Miami. I said I'd try to rent a car and that I'd let her know if I could, and when I'd pick her up. And then — "

Then, she said, she had walked back to the

hotel and gone up and changed and —

"Mrs. Payne," Jefferson said, "it didn't occur to you — not any time — to call the police? Tell them you had found a man stabbed to death? Particularly as you'd satisfied yourself your mother wasn't the one who had stabbed him?"

"When I got back," she said, "there were men at the end of the pier. And police cars in front. So the police knew. There wasn't anything I could tell them."

So she had arranged to rent the car, and telephoned her mother to be ready, and picked her up and —

"And the rest," she said, "was just the way I said it was. She checked in at the Columbus and we had lunch and I drove around and then came back."

She had, Pam realized, been speaking with growing confidence. It was as if she had been walking in fog, and come to a place where the fog was thinner, and walked more briskly, and came finally to a place where the air was clear.

Jefferson said he saw. He said, "Far's you know, your mother's at the Columbus now?"

"Why," she said, "yes. Anyway, I suppose she is. Unless — sometimes she does things on impulse."

Jefferson said, "Sure." He said, "I'll just

give them a ring and — " He stood up and looked down at the girl.

He turned, and started to walk away. And then Rebecca Payne said, "It's no good, is it? She won't be there. They'll tell you that. And — that she never registered there."

Jefferson came back and sat down again.

"All right, Mrs. Payne," Ronald Jefferson said. "Want to give it another try?"

"She didn't kill him," Rebecca said. "I know she didn't. She — she said I was crazy to think she had. She said she often got up early and went for a swim. That was all it was. I know that was all it was."

And she doesn't know, Pam North thought. She doesn't know at all.

XV

Chief Deputy Sheriff Ronald Jefferson had left, abruptly, to find a telephone. He had said, "Wait here, will you?" to the Norths, to Rebecca Payne. They had waited there, in the shady corner of the wide, long porch. Rebecca had put her hands, again, over her eyes, her fingers pressed hard against her forehead.

Four stories now, Pam thought, and each admitting something explicitly, or by implication, denied in the one which had preceded it. A drive alone to Miami, for the ride only, for distraction and for "thinking things out"; the same drive, equally innocent, with her mother, at her mother's request; once more a drive across the bridges, over varicolored waters, but this time with knowledge, and almost certainly with fear, as companions in the car. And now, this last.

There was not much difference in the last — only the vital difference which changed understandable evasion into flight. It had not taken the dark girl many words to have her other "try at it." She had spoken in a monotone, looking at nobody, looking toward the ocean.

It had been as she said until she reached

the motel. Then —

"She wasn't there," Rebecca said, in the dull voice, the voice without inflection. "I waited — oh, fifteen minutes. Perhaps longer. Then she came. She was wearing a bathing suit. It was wet. She said she had wakened early and gone for a dip, and then had breakfast. Only . . ."

She paused, then. After a moment, Jefferson said, "You didn't believe her, Mrs. Payne?"

"It . . ." the dark girl said, and paused again. "It wasn't like her. She almost never got up early. As for going for what she called a 'dip.' " Again she stopped. This time she resumed without prompting. "She's been sick," she said. "Her mind — it could have been more serious than they thought. If that was it — if she's really sick that way — they couldn't do anything to her, could they?"

There were things "they" could do, and would do if what Rebecca feared, was not quite saying, was true.

"It would be taken into account," Jefferson said. "You — what did you say to her when she came in?"

Rebecca had told her mother that Dr. Piersal was dead, and how he had died. Her mother had seemed shocked.

"Then it — what I was afraid of — got through to her and she was — seemed — incredulous and — and very angry. She said I must be crazy to think a thing like that. That I, not she, should be — she said — 'locked up somewhere.'"

"And, specifically, denied she had killed the doctor?"

"Over and over. With — with a kind of violence. It — she got more and more violent."

"You didn't believe her?"

"I . . ." She paused for a longer time, and looked at nobody. "I was afraid," she said. "I didn't know what to believe. Can't you understand how I felt? How — how dreadful it was?"

"Yes," Jefferson said. "You were the one who suggested she get away?"

Rebecca nodded her head, still not looking at him, not looking at the Norths.

"At first she said she wouldn't. That she had nothing to run away from, had not done anything. She said that — both things — several times. I tried to calm her down. Said I knew she hadn't. But that, anyway, it might be better. I said, 'It'll just be a mess if you stay here. There'll be all sorts of bothering things.' I told her it would be upsetting, and that there would be stories in the newspapers. Stories dragging up everything. I said there would be no use in going through all that. She calmed down finally and said that perhaps I was right."

She had got the car; they had driven to Miami. They had even had lunch at the "Top of the Columbus." But Mrs. Coleman had not checked in at the Columbus. By that time, Rebecca had persuaded her mother to go back to New York.

"I pretended I tried to get plane reservations," Rebecca said. "Said I couldn't. I don't know whether I could have or not but — but on planes there's a passenger list. People's names."

She had, instead, tried both railroads, and found a bedroom available on the afternoon Seaboard train. There had been, then, a momentary hitch. "It sounds ridiculous," Rebecca said. "She said she couldn't possibly ride in a bedroom. That I should know better than to expect her to. If I couldn't get a drawing room, well, she'd go in a compartment. But she wasn't going to be — 'cooped up,' she said — in a bedroom." The girl paused. "It was a double bedroom," she said. "Meant for two people."

It had taken a good deal of persuasion, many repetitions of how much of a nuisance it would be to be involved in the investigation of Dr. Piersal's death. But finally Mrs. Coleman had consented to the cooping up. Rebecca had waited until the long silvery train pulled out of the station, on the chance her mother might at the last minute change her mind.

"Then I did the things I said I did," Rebecca said. "Drove around, had my hair done in one of the Miami Beach hotels, came back here — "

It had been then that, abruptly, Jefferson had stood up and said, "Wait here, please," and gone into the hotel. He was gone about ten minutes.

"Got that friend of yours," he said, to the Norths. "Seemed the quickest way. There isn't much time to get organized. You want to say anything more, Mrs. Payne?"

"That's the way it was," she said, without taking her hands down from her face.

"You got your hair done, I suppose, in the hope the beachboy wouldn't recognize you."

"I suppose so," she said. "Does it make any difference?"

"I guess not," Jefferson said. "If you have any plans to leave town — "

"I haven't any plans for anything," the girl said. "Have I told you enough, now?"

"For now," Jefferson said, and the girl got up and walked down the long porch and into the hotel.

"They'll meet the train," Jefferson said, and sat down and lighted a cigarette. "Pick Mrs. Coleman up for questioning. If she hasn't got

237

off the train earlier. That train stops a lot of places. She could have got off damn near anywhere. You think she told the truth, finally?"

The Norths looked at each other. Jerry shrugged his shoulders. "I don't know," Pam said. "So many . . . variations."

"She could," Jefferson said, "have seen her mother stab him. Or not actually seen that, but seen her mother near — maybe on the pier, running."

"I suppose so," Pam said. "What happened to Bradley? His alibi stand up?"

"No," Jefferson said. "But it was for something else, apparently. A small-time con game. And, damn it to hell — I'm sorry ma'am — the con game gave him an alibi for the killing."

"Inconvenient," Jerry said.

"The double-crossing little so-and-so," Jefferson said. "Come to that, she could have killed him herself. Mrs. Payne. And dragged her mother into it, not the other way round."

"She's here," Pam pointed out. "She didn't run."

"Could be bluff. She did a lot of lying."

There was no arguing that, and neither North tried to argue it.

"How," Pam said, and now she was regarding the ocean, and might have been talking to herself, "did Mrs. Coleman know where to find him? Know he'd be at the end of the pier?"

"He'd be in plain sight," Jefferson said. "While he was standing up, anyway."

"To anyone here, staying at the hotel," Pam said. "Who happened to be up and about. Or who was looking for him. But she didn't stay here, did she? Walk blocks at the crack of dawn in a bathing suit on the chance that he might be out at the end of the pier? Or anywhere but asleep in bed?"

"She could have told him," Jefferson said. "Maybe they met at the dog races and he — oh, told her about these pelicans. I don't know. Anyway, it looks like she did know." He paused. "Somehow," he said.

Pam nodded her head, but continued to look at the ocean. Jerry looked at his wife. Whatever was on the tip of her mind was troubling it again, he decided.

"Hippocratic," Pam said absently and apparently to the Atlantic Ocean.

Jefferson looked at Jerry North quickly, obviously seeking translation. Jerry looked at his wife, and she looked at the Atlantic. They had, momentarily, achieved stalemate. Jerry ran fingers through his hair, without profit. He said, "Yes, Pam?"

"Oh," she said, "nothing. It kept coming out 'hypocritical' but I knew that wasn't right, of course."

Jerry searched his mind quickly. He said,

"Something in a crossword?"

Pam turned and looked at him, in evident surprise. She said, "Of course not, Jerry," and watched him raise baffled shoulders. "It's nothing," Pam said. "Just something I couldn't quite remember, and almost could. It gets to be a kind of itching."

Jerry knew the feeling. He said, "Oh," and then, "Was that what was on the tip of your mind?"

Pam looked toward, rather than at, him. It was clear she was re-examining her mind.

"I think so," she said, after some seconds of examination. "But only part of it. It feels like . . ." She paused. "Like a symbol of it," she said. "The oath that doctors take, you know."

Jerry said "Yes," and Jefferson, while still looking puzzled, looked relieved.

"Probably it will come to me," Pam said, reassuring everybody.

They waited briefly as was no more than polite.

"Eventually," Pam said.

Ronald Jefferson said, "Well." He said that he'd better go back to the office and stand by in case the New York police picked up Mrs. Coleman and — And then he stopped abruptly, and now it was he who looked abstractedly at the Atlantic. Then he sat down again. He said, "I've just had the craziest dam-fool idea. Suppose they did it together. And that Mrs. Coleman was never here at all."

He looked at them. They looked at each other. It was Jerry who said, "But — at the motel they — "

"Look," Jefferson said. "I said it's crazy. But, mothers and daughters look alike, some-times. According to this description your friend wired, Mrs. Coleman is slim and has black hair. And so's her daughter. O.K.?"

"Well — " Pam said.

"All right," Jefferson said, "like I said be-fore, it's crazy. But — suppose they decide, together, to knock off the doctor. Mrs. Cole-man gets out of this booby — this sanitarium — and goes to her apartment. But she leaves it. A week ago. You can go a hell of a long ways in a week, if you want to hide out. Mrs. Payne comes down here. She checked in Wednesday. Spotted Dr. Piersal. They'd al-ready known he'd be here. So, Friday she puts on suitable clothes — the kind a woman would wear to fly down in — maybe something of her mother's she's brought along for the pur-pose — and drives to the airport and waits until the morning plane comes in and parks her car and gets a cab and goes to The Bougainvillia and checks in as her mother. Wouldn't be any great trick after that to be her mother there and herself here, because nobody pays any attention to where hotel guests are. I mean, the management doesn't."

He paused, and looked expectant.

It was Jerry's turn to say, "Well." He added, "I suppose it could be done, but — "

"Kills Dr. Piersal," Jefferson said. "Gets the car. Checks out of the motel as Mrs. Coleman. Drives — "

"The bellboy — " Pam said.

"It would be easy enough to fix the bellboy," Jefferson said. "Be in the bathroom, say, when he comes for the bags. Tell him to take them down and put them in the car. Go down through the motel — you can do that, too, there — and come through and get in the car — Oh, it could be worked. Drive up to Miami and just kill enough time and come back and — well, and let us drag this rigmarole out of her. Making it hard but not too hard. So now — now we're chasing mama all over the place, but mama's already holed up, with a nice new name. If we do catch up with mama — well, she's not mentally responsible. As Mrs. Payne went to the trouble to mention. If we don't — well, when she figures it's safe, Mrs. Payne joins her and — "

Pamela North snapped her fingers. She said, "Of *course*. How stupid of me."

They both looked at her, both with surprise. Jefferson's surprise was, in fact, close to astonishment. Even as he was explaining it, and more with each word of explanation, it had seemed a pretty cockeyed notion. And here Mrs. North was —

"You mean to say," Jerry said, "you think this — this elaborate conspiracy — and it's full of holes anyway — is — "

"Oh," Pam said. "That." She shrugged her shoulders, and it occurred to Jefferson that she shrugged "that" from them. "No." She looked at Jefferson. "Not," she said, "that it isn't very ingenious. But . . ."

She stood up.

"I think," Pam North said, "that the first thing we'd better do is go to the library. Just to make sure. I think we'd all better go."

They looked at her, neither rising.

"Come *on*," Pam said. "I'll tell you on the way."

They stood up.

"Listen," Jerry said. "Just one thing. Has this anything to do with the Hippocratic oath?"

"Oh," Pam said, "not directly, of course. I don't suppose there's anything about it in that. It just got mixed up with that. In the dream, you know."

Jerry felt that he was in one. . . .

The woman at the reference desk was small

and spare and severe. She reminded Jerry of an English teacher who, many years ago, had taken the dimmest possible view of hanging participles and of many things, including, he had always felt, Gerald North. The same rimless eyeglasses; the same frosty gaze through them. Jerry felt himself shrinking into boyhood.

"We want a poison book," Pam said. It might, Jerry thought, have been "We want a cookbook." Miss — what had been the name? Miss Reid, that was it. Miss Reid would not have approved.

The librarian repeated, "A poison book?" and she sounded like Miss Reid — precise, but frosty. (As if an infinitive had wantonly been split.)

Jerry stood on one side of Pam at the counter; Deputy Sheriff Ronald Jefferson stood on her other side. The librarian looked at Jefferson. She said "Ronald?" as to a smallish boy. (A boy who had left a verb out of a sentence.)

Jefferson said, "Yes'm, Miss Phipps. This is Mrs. North. And Mr. North."

Miss Phipps did not say, "Indeed?" She merely looked "Indeed?"

She said, "A *poison* book?"

Jefferson looked at Gerald North, who quit revising long-ago themes and returned to the present.

"Toxicology," he said. "A book on pathology."

Miss Phipps said, "Really," putting the word at the end of a long pole. She looked again at Ronald Jefferson. He said, "Please, Miss Phipps."

" 'Legal Medicine, Pathology and Toxicology,' " Miss Phipps said. "By Gonzales, Vance, Helpern and Umberger."*

"That," Jerry said, "sounds fine."

"I suppose so," Miss Phipps said. "If you wish to sign for it, Ronald."

Ronald Jefferson said, "Surely."

It was a solid book, in greenish boards. They put it on a table and pulled chairs around it, and Pam opened it at random. She opened it, unfortunately, to a photographic illustration entitled: "Multiple suicidal stab wounds administered with a pocket knife." Pam said, "Ugh," and turned quickly to the index. She returned, this time with caution, to Page 833. There was no illustration on Page 833. (There was a small illustration on the facing page, which had to do with sulfadiazine crystals, but it was not especially alarming.)

"Digitalis," Pam read, keeping her voice at low, or library, pitch. "Powdered leaves of *Digitalis* something I can't pronounce or fox-

* And published by Appleton-Century-Crofts, Inc. New York.

glove. And so forth and so forth. And — here."
She pointed a finger. Jerry and Ronald Jefferson read, each over a Pam North shoulder:

"The symptoms of digitalis poisoning are slowing of the heart beat, 25 to 40 per minute, nausea, persistent vomiting, thirst, abdominal pain, suppression of urine, diarrhea, roaring in the ears, disturbance of vision, headache, hallucinations and delirium. Later the heart action becomes rapid and irregular, and is accompanied by dyspnea and collapse. Death may occur in convulsions and coma, or sudden cardiac failure may supervene."

"More or less what Doc Meister — " Jefferson said.

"Up to a point," Jerry said, at the same time, "the same symptoms from food poisoning or just a violent — "

Pam's finger moved on down the page. It stopped and tapped its nail.

"Fatal cases of digitalis poisoning are rare with fractionated doses since vomiting and diarrhea would tend to prevent further absorption," they read, and the moving finger descended the page and tapped again. "Fatalities are more apt to occur after intravenous injection of large dose of digitalis or strophanthin. In fatal poisoning death may occur after 1 or 2 days or not until 5 to 13 days have elapsed."

"Intravenous," Jefferson said. "It still could have been — Dr. Piersal could have made — It's probably the sort of drug doctors carry in their bags for — "

Pam turned the page, and again her finger moved down it; again the finger stopped, and the pink nail tapped.

"The determination of digitalis poisoning at autopsy presents great difficulties in the absence of a history revealing the quantity of the drug administered. . . . If death occurred as a result of an overdose of digitalis during its therapeutic administration for heart disease, this could hardly be established at autopsy."

They read on, although there was not much further on to read. Pam did say, "How awful," but that was when she read that cats were used, along with frogs, "to standardize preparation of digitalis for medicinal use."

"I'm sorry even about frogs," Pam said, "but *cats* — "

She closed the book, putting Drs. Gonzales, Vance, Helpern and Umberger in their places. Then she turned to face the two men and said, "Well?"

"It's still more or less what Dr. Meister said," Jefferson said, and spoke slowly. "Except — a fractionated dose could be a tablet, I suppose?"

They both supposed it could.

"Dr. Piersal could, I suppose, have made a mistake," Jerry said, and heard no conviction in his own voice. "It only says that fatal cases are 'rare' from fractionated doses. Not that they — "

It occurred to him that both Pam and Deputy Sheriff Jefferson had already read what he was about to remember for them.

"And Dr. Piersal could have injected the stuff intentionally," Pam said. "And we can find other bushes to beat around. But — Mr. Jefferson, Dr. Upton did say he'd given his wife her usual shot of insulin before he left Saturday morning."

"Yes."

"And Dr. Meister said she probably was taking insulin twice a day? So she probably gave herself another injection in the evening?"

"I suppose so. But we've nothing really to — "

"Oh," Pam said, "yes. Enough to start, I think."

They returned the book to Miss Phipps, who sniffed slightly and took it to an apparently distant shelf. They went out into the heat of late afternoon.

They went to Jefferson's office. It was hot, but it was private, and there were chairs to sit on.

There was also a message from the New York Police Department. The Seaboard's "Silver Comet" had arrived, more or less on time. If Mrs. Peter Coleman was on it, they had missed her on the dark arrival platforms. If she had been on it, she had declined to respond to paging on the public address system. Detectives had ridden on with the empty train to the Sunnyside yards, and Pullman porters were being questioned. Sometimes they remember passengers and sometimes they don't, and most often it is merely "maybe."

"Everything ends up in the air," Jefferson said, morosely.

They considered this for some time in silence. It was Pam who broke the silence.

"There's something we could try," Pam said. "It isn't very ethical, but murder isn't either. Suppose — "

XVI

Dr. Tucker Upton, asked if he could spare a few minutes, was resigned to it — his whole attitude was, Ronald Jefferson thought, one of almost numb resignation. Nothing mattered much, one way or the other. He said the autopsy was taking a long time and added, "For something which will come to nothing." Jefferson apologized for that; said that the pathologist had been delayed in getting started; added that Dr. Meister was getting along in years and probably wasn't as fast as he had been. He was also very thorough, a man not to be hurried.

"It doesn't matter," Upton said, in the tone of a man to whom nothing mattered. "I've canceled appointments for the rest of the week. It's only — well, it's the sort of thing one wants over."

Jefferson understood that. He was sorry to bother the doctor again. But —

"It's the Piersal business," he said. "It's still got us licked. Got me licked. I guess I need all the help I can get."

"Anything I can do," Dr. Upton said. "I can't imagine what. I didn't know him, except by reputation. I keep telling you that."

But there was still resignation, not asperity, in his voice.

"It's in connection with his treating your wife," Jefferson said, and Dr. Upton sighed and said, "Not that again, surely. We went over that."

They were in Paul Grogan's private office, which was air-conditioned. Even now, at nine in the evening, the air-conditioning was welcome.

"Something new's come — " Jefferson said, and there was knocking at the closed door. "Yes?" Jefferson said.

It was Pam North who opened the door. Jerry North was behind her. Pam said that Mr. Grogan had said he wanted to see them.

"Yes," Jefferson said. And, to Dr. Upton, "Hope you don't mind, doctor."

Upton's expression remained that of a man who didn't mind anything, and wasn't much interested in anything.

"Mr. and Mrs. North," Jefferson said. "Mr. North's connected with the New York police. Unofficially, that is. I've been — call it picking his brains. And his wife's. Mind if they sit in, doctor?" To the Norths, "This is Dr. Upton."

Upton said, "Why should I mind?"

Pam said, "We were so sorry about — " and Upton nodded his head slowly, cutting

251

that off. A man who had had enough of that, of all that was obvious and didn't matter.

The office was large. Jefferson sat behind Grogan's desk and Upton at the end of it. Pam and Jerry sat on a leather-covered sofa. The air-conditioning unit hummed softly. Over it, through the closed windows and faintly, there was sound of music from the patio.

"This has turned up," Jefferson said, and took an envelope out of his pocket. "Missed it the first time." He handed the envelope, which was empty, to Dr. Upton, who looked at it. It was addressed to Dr. Edmund Piersal, at The Coral Isles; it was postmarked New York. "Other side," Jefferson said, and Upton turned it over. "Seems to be about your wife, doctor."

There were penciled notations on the back of the envelope. Upton looked at them carefully; looked several times. Then he looked up at Deputy Sheriff Jefferson and waited.

"Made a copy," Jefferson said, and took a sheet of paper from his pocket and laid it on the desk in front of him. "Thought we might go over it together. Doesn't make much sense to me. But it does seem to be about your wife. 'Re Mrs. U.' "

"It would seem to be," Dr. Upton said, and again read the notations on the back of the envelope. "You're back on that, sheriff? That

Piersal did something wrong and killed himself because of that?"

His voice didn't change much. It did suggest weary surprise, but, with it, forbearance.

"To be honest," Jefferson said, "we're up in the air."

He did, Pam thought, sound very honest indeed; very much like a man up in the air.

Jefferson studied the notations in front of him. The lines he studied read:

"Re Mrs. U. Sl ovds dig? Symp comp. 9 pm impr inj ins her req hs prep hypo ck hs dos dig."

" 'Re Mrs. U.' " Jefferson said. "That's clear enough, isn't it?"

He looked at Dr. Upton for agreement; Upton was studying the notations, but nodded his head.

"In the other notes," Jefferson said, " 'sl' meant slow. Anyway, we thought it did. But 'sl ovds dig' with a question mark. Slow what would you guess, doctor?"

Dr. Upton evidently gave the matter thought.

"Looks," Jefferson said, "like he was guessing about something, doesn't it?"

"It could be," Upton said, after a further pause, "that he was speculating as to whether my poor wife had taken a slight overdose of digitalis. She told him she was taking it. The 'symp comp' could mean symptoms compatible, of course. They would be, to some degree. Nausea. Slowing of the heart beat."

"That's probably it," Jefferson said. "It had us licked." He turned to the Norths. He said, "See? I figured he would help us."

"Only," Pam said, discouragement in her tone, "it doesn't seem to get us any place, does it?"

"Guess not," Jefferson said. "She was taking digitalis, doctor?"

"As I told you," Upton said. "One fifteen-hundredth of a milligram tablet a day. Maintenance dose. Couldn't harm her."

"If she got confused. Took more."

"Throw it up," Upton said. "Before it did any real harm."

Jefferson sighed. He said he guessed they weren't getting anywhere. However —

"The next thing," he said. " '9 pm impr.' Suppose that means he went back at nine Saturday evening and found her improved?"

"Could mean that," Dr. Upton said. "Would have been, I'd think. Probably half asleep. Dramamine does that, in large enough doses."

"The next? 'Inj ins her req?' If that's a grouping."

"Probably," Upton said, "she asked him to give her the shot of insulin which was due about then. I told you, she hated to do it herself." He sighed. "The poor thing," he said. "The poor, unhappy woman. Knew she had to have it to stay alive and — and dreaded it so she'd sometimes — well, she'd say she forgot it." He sighed again. "Lots of people are like that," he said. "If patients do half what you tell them to do . . ."

He did not finish that. Jefferson gave him time, but he seemed, again, to have gone far away, gone into the blankness of his inner life.

" 'Hs prep hypo,' " Jefferson read. "Comes right after the bit about her request, if that's what it was. Mean anything to you, doctor?"

Dr. Upton looked at the notes again, looked up at Jefferson, said, "Can't say it does, sheriff."

"It didn't to us either," Pam North said. "But then, so little of it — wait a minute!

"In the other notes," Pam said, and spoke quickly, as if to get words out before an idea slipped away. "In the notes in the notebook, 'hs' meant you, doctor. That is, we decided it meant 'husband.' And this time — couldn't it read, 'husband prepared hypodermic?' That is, for the insulin shot. And — did you, doctor?"

"Yes," Dr. Upton said. "I usually did. To make sure of the right number of units."

"This other medication," Pam said. "Dramamine or whatever it was. It wouldn't be — incompatible with the insulin shot? Or — contra — what's the rest of it? Of course. Contraindicated because she'd been sick?"

"She asked that," Dr. Upton said. "Looking — looking for an excuse. I told her that he was a doctor. Wouldn't use anything incompatible with insulin since he knew she was on it."

"I guess this isn't getting us anywhere, Dr. Upton," Jefferson said. "As for the last — "

The door of the office opened, with no preliminary knocking. A slim dark woman in a dark linen suit stood in the doorway.

"You're this sheriff," she said, her voice high, excited. "What have you been doing to my baby?"

They turned and looked at her. They looked at her blankly. Paul Grogan appeared behind her and shook his head and spread his hands, indicating hopelessness; indicating he had tried and failed.

"Becky," she said. "You've been hounding Becky."

"I don't — " Jefferson said.

"I've come back to stop that," the woman said. "I've brought Tony with me. It won't be just defenseless women any more. I've — why, hello!"

The last appeared to be addressed to Dr. Tucker Upton, who appeared to look surprised.

"I'm amazed," the slender, black-haired woman — the woman who did, in fact, look not a little like her daughter — said. "I'm really *amazed*. You actually *found* him!"

We had it in hand, Pam North thought; I really thought we had it in hand. And now — *this!*

"I suppose," Jefferson said, and there was a kind of wariness in his tone, "that you're Mrs. Coleman?"

"Of course I'm Mrs. Coleman. Who did you think I was?"

Several appropriate answers occurred to Gerald North. "Avenging fury" was among them.

"I suppose," Mrs. Coleman said, "that this gentleman — I heard you say Dr. Upton? — has told you?"

Jefferson looked at Upton, who was looking, it seemed rather fixedly, at Mrs. Peter Coleman. Upton appeared to become conscious that Jefferson was looking at him. He looked at Jefferson, and raised his eyebrows and shook his head.

"About what, Mrs. Coleman?" Deputy Sheriff Jefferson said, as patiently as he could.

"The beach bag, of course," she said, with no patience at all. "What did you think I was talking about? About helping me pick things up and being so nice after I caught the beach bag — "

She stopped, as if she had stumbled over something incomprehensible.

"I don't understand at all," she said. "Isn't that why he's — why you're questioning him?"

Jefferson looked again at Dr. Upton.

"I'm sorry," Upton said. "I haven't the least idea what she's talking about."

"The beach place," Mrs. Coleman said. She spoke slowly and distinctly, as if to a very backward child. "The place called the 'Sun and Surf'. I caught my beach bag on the corner of a table and it spilled everything and you were just coming in for breakfast and helped me pick things up. Of course you remember." She looked at Dr. Upton. "Of course you do," she said.

"I'm sorry," Upton said. "I'm afraid you've got me confused with somebody else."

"I," Mrs. Coleman said, "do not forget faces, Dr. Upton. Anybody can tell you that."

It was entirely out of hand, Pam North thought. She reached for it.

"Mrs. Coleman," Pam said, "when was this?"

Mrs. Coleman looked at Pam as if, for the first time, she was conscious of her presence in the room.

"I," Pam said, "am Mrs. Gerald North. This

is my husband."

She indicated her husband.

"Mrs. North," Mrs. Coleman said, accept-ingly. "Mr. North. What did you say?"

"When — "

"Why, yesterday morning, of course," Mrs. Coleman said. "At a little after seven. I'd gone for an early dip and then had a cup of coffee and toast — I never eat much breakfast — and caught my bag when I was going out. You know how it is, my dear — sun glasses, sunburn lotion, comb, reading glasses — so many things. And when I got back to the motel my daughter — my own daughter — didn't believe me. Oh, she didn't say so. Not in so many words. But I could tell — "

She stopped abruptly.

"Why," she said, "are you all looking at me like that?"

"Yesterday morning?" Jefferson said. "At a little after seven? Yesterday?"

"How many times?" Mrs. Coleman said. "He was wearing bathing trunks and a beach coat, like everybody does there all the time. It's a very informal place and — "

"Well, Dr. Upton?" Jefferson said.

"I never saw Mrs. Coleman before in my life," Tucker Upton said, his voice heavy. "At that hour, sheriff, I was on U.S. 1, some-where between Miami and Homestead. Probably nearer Miami. I got here about ten and found — "

"I know," Jefferson said. "You told me. You're sure, Mrs. Coleman?"

"Of course I'm sure," Mrs. Coleman said. "I've no idea why he denies it. I — *oh!*"

"Yes," Jefferson said, "it was at a little before seven yesterday morning, Mrs. Coleman, that Dr. Piersal was killed. And that's why you wanted to make it so clear you were at the Sun and Surf, isn't it?"

"But I was there. You don't listen. I woke early and it was a beautiful morning and I decided to go for a dip. People at the motel have beach privileges at the Sun and Surf, you know. It's supposed to be a club — "

"I know," Jefferson said. "When was this?"

"About six-thirty. So I had my dip and then coffee and toast and then, when I was going out, there was this about the bag and this gentleman — yes, *you* — helped me and — "

"Mrs. Coleman," Pam said, "did you know Dr. Upton was here? Before you came in? Mr. Grogan tried to stop you, didn't he? Didn't he tell you Dr. Upton was here?"

Mrs. Coleman looked at Pam North, and looked from her to Ronald Jefferson, and then raised her eyebrows.

"All right," Jefferson said. "Consider I've asked the same things. Officially. And that

260

Paul Grogan is an old friend of mine and — "

"I don't," Mrs. Coleman said, "see what difference it makes. For all I knew, he — " she pointed at Jerry North — "might just as well have been Dr. Upton. What you're trying to say is — "

She looked at Jefferson and said, "Well?"

"Dr. Upton," Jefferson said, "has an alibi for the murder of Dr. Piersal. If he needs one. But if he was here in Key West at that hour, and only a few blocks from here, his alibi is shot, isn't it? At the same time, you yourself have an alibi of sorts. If you were going out when he came in you were there earlier. Perhaps at the time Dr. Piersal was being killed."

"This," Mrs. Coleman said, and now there was neither excitement nor stridency in her voice, "is the man who helped me pick things up. It was at about seven-fifteen yesterday morning. At the Sun and Surf, which is about ten minutes' walk from here."

"I," Dr. Upton said, "never saw this woman before in my life. I don't question her account of what happened. No doubt she'll be able to find the man who did help her. But it wasn't I."

And then he started to stand up. He said, "For your information, deputy sheriff, the last notations undoubtedly mean 'check with husband as to digitalis dosage.' And that, I'm afraid, is all the help — " He stood up. "I've

261

told you the dosage. Fifteen hundredths of a milligram daily. I — "

"Won't keep you long, doctor," Jefferson said. "Still — perhaps you can help us clear up this confusion. So — "

He looked at Dr. Upton's chair. Dr. Upton hesitated, then sat down again.

He didn't, Pam thought, look so far away now, so deep within himself, in the loneliness of his mind.

"Mrs. Coleman," Jefferson said, "your daughter drove you to Miami. Put you on a train for New York."

"That's just it," Mrs. Coleman said. "Helping a fugitive to escape. I realized that. So when we got to Washington, I got off and called Tony up, and told him. And we decided to come right back. So you wouldn't hound her."

"I see," Jefferson said. "Who is this Tony?"

"Why," Mrs. Coleman said, "Becky's husband, of course. He's been half out of his mind worrying about her."

Half out of my mind is about where I'm getting to be, Jerry thought.

"You weren't a fugitive," Jefferson said. "There was no charge against you. There isn't now. Why did you agree to — run?"

"Because I didn't want to get mixed up in it," Mrs. Coleman said. "Oh, I said things

262

about Dr. Piersal. That was a long time ago and I didn't mean them but — Oh, I didn't think clearly. Sometimes I — sometimes I don't. Becky thinks she's got a poor crazy mother and — and that's what makes her afraid. Afraid she'll be like me. That's why she left Tony. Got all mixed up. Only I'm not, really. Anyway, I realized after a while that I was leaving *Becky* mixed up in it, so of course I got hold of Tony and we came back." She looked at Dr. Upton. "And whatever you say," she said, "you were at the Sun and Surf yesterday morning, not on U.S. 1 somewhere."

Upton did not bother to look at her. He merely sighed.

"I was wearing a white bathing suit," Mrs. Coleman said. "With a blue beach jacket over it."

She seemed to be trying to help the dark-clad, remote man remember something he had forgotten. It was as if, once he remembered, he would think better of his denial. She seemed to be entirely unprepared for the deep silence which greeted what she had said; for Jefferson and the Norths to look at her with such new intentness. After a few seconds she said, "Did I say something that — ?"

"Mrs. Coleman," Jefferson said, "when your daughter came to find you. After she

263

had found Dr. Piersal's body. What was she wearing?"

"Why," Mrs. Coleman said, "the same — why do you ask me that? What difference does it — ?"

"White bathing suit with a blue jacket?" Jefferson said. "Very like what you were wearing?"

"Not very like," Mrs. Coleman said. "Exactly like. I bought myself a suit and jacket last summer. They were matching, you know. The suit has blue decorations. Matches the jacket. Little darts down the — "

"Yes," Jefferson said. "And — "

"And I bought Rebecca one too," she said. "We're the same size. Sometimes people can hardly believe we're really mother and — "

"Mrs. Coleman," Jefferson said, and his voice was heavy. "The woman who was seen — seen by a beachboy, but you know that — running on the pier Sunday morning, running away from what she had found, was wearing what the boy took to be white shorts. *And* a blue jacket. Was the woman you, Mrs. Coleman? You, not your daughter?"

She looked at him. Her perfectly applied mouth opened slightly.

"Why," Mrs. Coleman said, "what a dreadful thing to say. What a really *dread*ful thing!"

XVII

It's all going wrong, Pam North thought — going "dreadfully" wrong. And I was so almost certain. Mrs. Coleman and her daughter together, after all? Not as Mr. Jefferson thought — not the farfetched way he thought. A way we're only now beginning to piece —

"Doctor," Jerry North said, "when did you first learn that Dr. Piersal had treated your wife on Saturday? Grogan told you after she died? That's what you told the deputy, isn't it?"

Jerry looked at Ronald Jefferson, who said, "Yes. That's what he told me."

"What's that got to do — ?" Upton said, his tone dull, uninterested. "Not that it matters. Yes, Grogan told me."

"A while ago," Jerry said, "you spoke as if you had talked to your wife about it. But she was dead when you arrived. You said something about her having asked if what Piersal had given her would be incompatible with her insulin shot. And you — let me see if I can remember it — you 'told her he was a doctor.' Wouldn't give her anything that was contraindicated for a person taking insulin. Don't you remember saying that?"

Jefferson looked at Jerry North, and his eyes

narrowed. And Pam looked at Jerry, and her eyes widened. There was time for this before Upton answered.

"Grogan told me," Upton said. "As I told the sheriff here. It's a — obviously a trivial point. I wasn't in a mood for trivial points. I'm not now, Mr. North. Or — absurd theories. That a man of Piersal's experience made a mistake of some sort. And killed himself because — good God, man."

His tone was very weary. He shook his head in tired rejection of the absurd. They waited.

"However," he said, "I knew Piersal had been asked to have a look at her, and had had a look at her. Knew this before Grogan told me. I telephoned my wife from my office in Miami Saturday afternoon. I usually did when we had to be separated. This stomach upset had started before I left Saturday. I called to ask how she was feeling. It was then she told me Piersal had been in and given her something, and she said she felt much better, and asked about the insulin shot — hoping I'd say she'd better not take it, poor Florence."

"You were surprised," Jerry said, "that Dr. Piersal had been called in? Not the hotel physician? Doctor — " He looked at Jefferson.

"Townsend," Jefferson said. "Were you, doctor?"

"I," Dr. Upton said, "was a little surprised anybody had been called in. These attacks of hers made her damned uncomfortable. But they weren't serious."

"This one was," Jefferson said.

"Her heart gave out," Upton said. "I keep telling you that. The autopsy will show that."

"Would it show if she had taken an overdose of digitalis? Enough to end her life?"

"She'd been taking digitalis," Upton said, his voice still weary, resigned. "I keep on telling you the same things over and over. As to the autopsy — no, probably not, in view of the maintenance doses she'd been taking. The recovery of digitalis from the organs is difficult."

As, Pam thought, somebody just said. No — wait a minute. As I just read, in the same words. In the book with the long name, by so many doctors. It's as if Dr. Upton had just —

"When you talked to her, doctor," Jefferson said, "how did she seem? I mean — depressed? Upset?"

"No," Upton said. "She sounded a little sleepy. Dramamine, if that's what he gave her, would have that effect."

"You told her?"

"To rest. To take her insulin when it was time for it. That I'd be back as soon as I could make it. That the operation I'd gone up to do had turned out a little more complicated than I'd expected, and that I would have to wait around a few hours. Be on hand if something went wrong." He paused, looked at Jefferson intently. "If what you're getting at," he said, "is did she sound depressed enough to take an overdose of digitalis, no she didn't. Of course . . ."

He paused.

"I thought she just sounded sleepy," he said. "I suppose — suppose it's possible — she was really deeply depressed. She had cause enough to be, poor Florence. The dullness in her voice — it might have been because nothing mattered to her any more and — " He broke off. He put his right hand over his eyes.

"About when was this, doctor? When you talked to her?"

"Around four o'clock. Some time between four and five."

Jefferson looked at him for a moment. Then Jefferson picked up the telephone and, after a moment, said "Sally?" Then he said, "Good. Were you on the board Saturday afternoon? Trying to check out on something — get a time straight. You remember a call coming through for Mrs. Upton? Mrs. Tucker Upton?" He listened a moment. "I know there isn't," he said. He covered the mouthpiece.

"Says there's no record kept of incoming calls," he said. "I — yes, Sally?"

He listened again. He said, "I see." He said, "Well — yes, I can see how it would." He said, "Thanks, Sally." He hung up.

He looked for some seconds at Dr. Tucker Upton. Then he said, "Doctor. When you got back here, went to your room — to the suite you and Mrs. Upton had on the ground floor — was there a 'Don't Disturb' sign on the door?"

Dr. Upton had taken away the hand which had shielded his eyes. He looked at Jefferson. There was no longer any dullness in his eyes.

"No," he said. "I don't remember there was."

There was no longer any dullness in his voice.

"Probably the maid will remember," Jefferson said. "They like to start as early as they can, you know."

"These trivial things," Dr. Upton said. "All right. I said I didn't remember. It could have been there. I could be wrong about it."

"Yes," Jefferson said. "I'm afraid you were, doctor. About — about quite a few things, come down to it. You see, after Dr. Piersal saw her, he left word at the desk that she wasn't to be disturbed. By telephone calls or anything else."

269

"I told the operator who I was," Upton said. "Obviously, it didn't apply — "

Jefferson shook his head slowly.

"No, doctor," he said. "Oh, I don't mean Sally — she's the girl on the board, you know — wouldn't have made an exception in your case. But, she's a very conscientious girl, doctor. Fixed in her mind not to put any calls through to your suite, you see. Made a special case of it, sort of. That's why she remembers, doctor. You see, the point never came up. Because there weren't any calls to put through, doctor. Not between four and five. Not any time."

"She forgot," Dr. Upton said. "Maybe she was relieved. Went off the board for a while."

"Oh, yes," Jefferson said. "One of the boys relieved her about six, for dinner. She told him not to let anyone bother poor Mrs. Upton. Everybody knew she wasn't well, doctor. Everybody was sorry for her. When she came back, he told her nobody had tried to bother poor Mrs. Upton."

He stopped. Upton said nothing.

"Want to have another try, doctor?" Jefferson said. "Or — want I should? Like your wife's not having died yet when you got back some time in the middle of the night? To see if things were going as you planned? If she'd died yet? Telling you then that Piersal had been to see her. Like your having to wait until she did die, from the second overdose of digitalis you'd left for her to inject, telling her it was insulin? As you did in the morning before you left. Must have come as a shock to you, doctor, to find that a man like Piersal had examined her, not poor old Doc Townsend, who'd just have given her bicarb."

Dr. Upton shook his head. He said that all this was preposterous; that, said before witnesses, it was slander. But he was tolerant. He realized Jefferson had to test out every theory, preposterous or not. He advised that Jefferson think this one through.

His tone was steady, reasonable.

"You see," he said, "Dr. Piersal *didn't* diagnose digitalis poisoning. Oh, a possible slight overdose. But that only as an outside possibility. You hadn't thought of that, apparently."

"Oh, yes," Pam North said. "We did think of that, doctor. But — he would have a quite different idea after she died, wouldn't he? Knowing she hadn't died of an upset stomach. And that a second injection of digitalis, on top of what she'd had — even if that was only a slight overdose added to her regular intake — might well have killed her. If — if he'd been alive to have any ideas at all. But he wasn't, was he, doctor? You saw to that. How did you find him, doctor? Go to his room first and when he wasn't there, go out looking for him? See him out at the end of the pier and go out, with a fisherman's knife in the pocket of your jacket? What did you say to him, doctor? Thank him for treating your wife? Or just say, 'Sorry, doctor. I guess you know too much'? Or didn't you say anything at all before you stabbed him?"

Upton put his hands on the arms of his chair and leaned forward as if he were about to stand up. But then he sank back into the chair. He said, "You're out of your minds. All of you. Out of your minds." His voice again was dull, uninflected.

"Look at yourself, Dr. Upton," Pam said. "At the way you're dressed. It's very suitable, isn't it? Suitable for a bereaved husband. But not for a place like this, is it, doctor? A — a fun place. A place for bright clothes."

He looked at her. His lips parted as if he were about to speak, but he did not speak.

"Why did you bring these clothes when you came back here, doctor?" Pam said. "These suitable clothes? It was because you knew you'd need them, wasn't it, doctor? Knew you'd have a role to play — the grieving husband role. Because — "

"Shut up," Upton said, and he spoke loudly, and did stand up now. "Damn you — shut up. I don't have to take this from some fool, meddling — "

But then he stopped speaking and looked at nothing, and spoke as if to himself.

"Why did he have to be here?" he asked the air around him. "Piersal of all the men in the world? Why the hell did he have to be here?"

The Norths, dressed for tennis, sat under an umbrella by the courts and waited. It was two-thirty on Tuesday afternoon. The opposition was somewhat late in arriving, but the Norths were in no special hurry.

"There's not much to take to court," Jerry said. "Not even with this woman in Miami Jefferson found out about. A telephone call Upton claimed he made, and didn't make. Mrs. Coleman's insistence he was at the Sun and Surf when he was supposed just to have left Miami on his way down. She won't be an especially good witness, Pam. Not with her history. Her — her obvious flightiness."

"His dark suit," Pam said. "Which was what was on the tip of my mind all the time. It got mixed up with the Hippocratic oath the way things do in dreams — that maybe there was something in the oath about doctors wearing seemly clothes. There isn't, incidentally. But that was just a dream. The fact that he quoted a sentence from that poison book —

quoted it exactly, as if he'd just looked it up and committed it to memory. And what he said at the end about Piersal. What we all heard him say."

"An expression of regret at the misfortune of a distinguished colleague," Jerry said. To which Pam said, with some vehemence, "Tommyrot."

"The autopsy doesn't show Mrs. Upton was murdered," Jerry said. "That he gave her an overdose of digitalis and arranged for her to give herself a second. The state certainly can't introduce the notes you and I and Jefferson concocted, dragging digitalis into it. We don't know that Piersal made that second visit. That was only our guessing."

"Yes," Pam said. "But a right guess, I think. Dr. Upton didn't deny it. He must have talked to his wife — learned that Piersal had been to see her — after nine o'clock. Since he was having dinner with this woman at The Columbus in Miami at eight. Mrs. Upton probably told him then that Piersal had made a second visit."

"A lot of 'probablys'," Jerry said. "I'd hate to be the prosecuting attorney. Try to convince a jury, for example, that Upton killed a man and then went on and had breakfast."

"Where he wasn't known," Pam said. "And he'd been up all night, waiting for his wife to die. Looked all over the place for Dr. Piersal, probably. Had a lot of other things to do — change into something he might have driven down from Miami in, be seen coming back into the hotel at the right time, act shock and bereavement. He needed to build up his strength. Also, you won't be the prosecuting attorney. And the defense will have some explaining to do."

She stopped, and looked away across the courts, not at anything in particular. Jerry waited.

"More explaining than it will be able to do," Pam said. "Oh — reasonable doubt. Perhaps. But — if anywhere, only in the minds of the jury, Jerry. Because they'll be responsible. But not in any other minds. Everybody will know, won't they? As we know. The county medical society, or whatever it is. And the hospital people. And — and all the people who might be patients. Oh — they may let him go on walking around. I doubt it, but they may. That'll be all he'll have left, won't it? Not really a doctor anymore. Just — just a man let walk around."

It seemed to Jerry that Pam shivered slightly, hearing her own words.

"The way Mr. Bradley is let walk around," Pam said, and turned to Jerry, and her eyes focused.

"Of course," she said, "maybe he'll confess. He almost did last night — in a way he *did* last night." She looked beyond Jerry. "Here they come," Pam North said.

Mrs. Peter Coleman and Mrs. Anthony Payne did, indeed, look a good bit alike, seen from a distance. They walked on either side of a tall, blond man, and Rebecca looked up at him, laughing, her face bright. When she said, "This is Tony, my husband," her voice was bright. "Isn't he beautiful?" Mrs. Coleman asked them and Tony looked down at her, and grinned, and said, "Cut that out, mother," and was glad to meet the Norths. He seemed an easy and confident man.

They played family against family, and on the court Tony Payne was easy and confident. And Rebecca Payne was not the embarrassed, insecure girl of the Saturday before. She and Tony ran with glee, made cheerful chirping sounds of encouragement and admiration at each other.

Whatever it had been, it had gone now, Pam thought. Probably Rebecca had thought it was going to be like mother, like daughter. People — nervous, imaginative people — get absurd notions. Anyway, there wasn't anything really wrong with Mrs. Coleman. A little fey, perhaps. So — apparently a happy ending, Pam thought, putting what was

276

meant to be a drop shot into the bottom of the net.

The Norths got clobbered.

THORNDIKE PRESS hopes you have enjoyed this Large Print book. All our Large Print titles are designed for easy reading, and all our books are made to last. Other Thorndike Large Print books are available at your library, through selected bookstores, or directly from the publisher. For more information about current and upcoming titles, please call or mail your name and address to:

THORNDIKE PRESS
PO Box 159
Thorndike, Maine 04986
800/223-6121
207/948-2962

X